The Cloak

By

James Hussey

An Original Publication from James Hussey

The Cloak
Written and published by James Hussey
Copyright © 2020 by James Hussey
All rights reserved.

To all those that helped me.

~ Chapter One ~

Christos had dreamt of it for many years. Now the days were drawing near when he would leave his life in the country and begin the adventure which he felt would weigh himself against the world. His passion had always been for drawing. He didn't know why he did it or wanted to do it, no one he knew did anything of the kind. The people he lived amongst rose before the sun and worked the fields and tended their animals till nightfall. The world of imagination and creation seemed not to hold sway over them as it did over him.

Christos had helped his mother from an early age on their small plot of land. He was her only child, and after the death of his father, when he was no more than a boy, he helped her tend the few chickens and goats and ploughed the meagre amount of land they had. But now that she too had passed away, he felt free to realise his dream, to be an artist.

The livestock, he sold off to neighbours at a generous price, and the land would be returned to the duke. The coins he had raised from the sale of the animals were not many, but from two of them, he had a new pair of boots made in green leather. He didn't feel they were a luxury as his journey to the city would take many days and the boots he had were on the verge of falling apart.

On the Sunday after church, the duke's man arrived on horseback as Christos had been told he would. He gave a cursory glance to the simple dwelling which had been Christos' home since birth but had no need of any detailed viewing. Christos knew the man well. He was fair and kind and the reasons for Christos leaving had become known. People thought him both courageous and foolish and his plan, his dream, had reached the duke, who had sent him a farewell gift of some wine, cheese, and bread, and best and most surprisingly, a sheaf of papers inside a leather folder. Christos asked for his gratitude to be relayed. The man nodded and with a smile, turned and rode away, leaving Christos standing outside what was no longer his home on the first morning of his adventure.

The day was warm with wind from the south. Christos stood, deep in reflection on the red-brown earth outside of what had once been his home. As he looked around, he felt himself somehow older. He knew every tree, bush and plant for miles around. The sky above was his sky, the clouds his friends, no matter what time of year, and he was leaving them, leaving it all behind for a dream, a desire. Were those who knew him right, was he being foolish? Doubt flickered across his mind, but as he looked at the distant hills nearly a day's walk away, his heart seemed to beat a little quicker, and his blood pulsed a little faster at the thought of what lay ahead.

He picked up his small bundle from the ground, to which he'd added the wine, cheese, and bread. It also contained some fruit, a flask of water, his other two shirts, leggings, a mat woven by his mother which was about as long as his height on which he would sleep, a coat made from goatskin, a small pouch tied with twine containing his money, some sticks of charcoal, six or seven drawings of plants and the sheaf of paper in its dark brown leather folder. Putting the bag over his shoulder he started off towards the distant hills.

By late afternoon, Christos had reached the summit of those hills. He was tired, perhaps more with the emotional strain than anything physical, but before he took a rest he turned and looked at where he had come from. Although he couldn't make out his house, by tracing the colour and shapes of the tapestry of fields and woods spread out below him he knew where it was. After a short pause, he turned and walked over the hilltop. Stopping under a tree that had wide branches, he opened his bag and ate and drank. As he reclined under the tree's canopy a crow hopped towards him and he shared some of his bread. Then he slept through till dawn.

When he awoke, it was still more dark than light. The moon was new, a slither of icy white pinned, it seemed, to the morning sky. Those first few moments of the new day the trees changed imperceptibly from blackish copper to dark green. After a sip of wine and the last of his bread, he set off down the hill.

It was now light. The land before him looked inviting and he wanted to make good progress as he had been told his journey to the city by the sea would take three to four days.

After a short while, Christos came upon the first person he had seen since leaving home. By the side of the road sat an old man smoking a pipe with a bundle of reeds tied with leather straps to his back. They exchanged a friendly morning greeting and Christos enquired as to how far it was to the nearest town.

"Oh, not far for someone with your youth and vigour, you will probably be there by late afternoon," the old man replied. Christos thanked him and wished him a good day and carried on his way. Then just before he was out of earshot, the old man called out, "Young man, don't forget to carry a good thought with you every day."

Some few hours later he reached his destination. He had been to towns of this size before but not often, and never this one. As he reached its boundary, people gave him a glance as they went about their daily routines. Christos was hungry and needed to buy food. The main street had stalls selling all manner of goods and foodstuffs, meats, fruits, bread, pies and foods he didn't even know. He bought some cooked chicken off a fat man with red cheeks, a small pebble-shaped loaf from a woman with orange hair and green eyes, and two apples out of a barrel from a boy who had been playing a game on the ground with glass balls and who seemed slightly irritated at having to stop the game to sell the fruit.

Happy with what he had bought, Christos wandered down the street. At a crossroad, he came across a fountain from which water spewed out of a stone lions head into a circular basin. People were sitting on its edge or were stopping around it to talk.

Christos watched the plume of water cascade from the lion's mouth creating droplets of rainbow colours as they entered the basin. His reverie was broken by laughter coming from his left, his eyes followed the sound to an open door where three men emerged into the street arms around one another. Above them, Christos saw a painted sign of a green fish, and underneath, the words Rooms to Rent.

He knew he had two more days of journeying to go to get to the city and although sleeping outdoors was no hardship, a bed for the night would be pleasant. Having seen a few dark clouds slip quietly into view, he knew rain would follow during the night, so he entered the inn of the Green Fish.

He went through the door the three men had just come out of to find a room that was large and rectangular, and painted pale green with a high ceiling. The room was full of smoke, with people mostly sitting at wooden tables talking, some quietly, some raucously. Others were playing cards or dice, while four men near the door were playing a game with metal tiles with dots on them and a board with rows of holes and pegs in some of the holes. Fifty or so people must have been in there, all men except for three women who carried trays of drinks and plates of food from the bar which was ahead of him and spanned the width of the room.

Sometimes the women would stay awhile at a table and sometimes sit on a man's lap which always produced more laughter.

Christos nervously made his way to the bar. The man behind it welcomed him and asked what he would like.

"A room for the night," he replied.

"Certainly, young man," the innkeeper said. "A room overlooking the street became vacant this morning, I will show you to it shortly but first would you like a drink?"

"Some wine," Christos replied and took his drink to an empty table in the corner.

After watching the comings and goings of the Green Fish for a while, Christos felt more at ease, the wine helping him to relax. He then took from his bag some paper and a stick of charcoal and began unnoticed, or so he thought, to sketch the different characters. First, he drew two men with a scrap of paper on the table between them that one kept jabbing his finger at. Then he drew a man asleep in the far corner with his mouth open and one also of the innkeeper going about his work. The daylight by now had faded and after a second cup of wine and a bowl of rabbit stew, brought to him by one of the women, Christos decided it was time to sleep. He wanted to rise early and make good progress in the morning.

Christos asked the innkeeper where his room was.

"On the first-floor, room seven with the yellow door. But before you retire, young sir, may I see your drawings? I couldn't help noticing."

Christos showed the innkeeper what he had drawn.

"They're wonderful!" the man exclaimed. "I'll make you an offer, let me keep these drawings, and your food, drink, and the night's stay are free, and breakfast too."

Christos smiled and, feeling slightly embarrassed, agreed.

9

He slept well that night, happy, especially as someone had thought what he had done was of value.

The first rays of sunlight illuminated the floorboards. Christos poured water from a pitcher into a bowl, splashing it on his face, dressed, tidied his bed and went downstairs.

The innkeeper was already at work helping bring in vegetables from a cart in the street. "Good morning," he cried, "I'll be with you soon."

"I'll help you," Christos replied.

Soon the cart was unloaded and had turned and trundled back to the countryside.

Over warm bread, sliced ham, and a nettle tea, the pair breakfasted together.

"Where are you heading?" the innkeeper inquired.

Christos told of his past and of his desire to be an artist, and how he hoped to find work in a master's studio in the city.

"Well I know little of such things," the innkeeper said, "but I thought the drawings you did last night were wonderful. You portrayed me and the others so well. But what I can tell you, as luck would have it, is that today in about an hour, a wagon stops here before going on to the city and it will be carrying precious earth which I believe is made into paint. I know the driver well, I'm sure he would let you ride with him, and it's possible he may be able to assist you with information as to where to begin your search."

As the innkeeper had said, about an hour later a wagon arrived, and almost immediately a boy appeared and took the horses away to the stables to feed and rest.

After greeting the innkeeper, the driver was introduced to Christos. He was a tall thin man with large hands and long dark hair tied with a black bow.

After listening to what the innkeeper had to tell him, he grinned broadly, showing a missing tooth. "No trouble, of course you can ride with me. My name is Giorgio and when the horses are rested, we'll go, and God willing we should be in the city before nightfall."

A couple of hours later the two set off.

"Tell me," Christos said, "The innkeeper said you were carrying precious earth, what is it?"

"About four days southwest, there is golden earth that artists in the city turn into paint. If ground smooth then mixed with oil or egg it becomes a beautiful yellow colour, and when heated to expel the water it darkens and takes on a reddish hue." Giorgio explained. "It's not the most valuable of colours but it's always in great demand and the moving of it has kept me in work for many years."

The wagon moved slowly on along the rutted roads. Cresting a hill, as the shadows began to lengthen, the city Christos had dreamt of came into sight. Shining and glittering on the edge of the sea. Nothing had prepared him for what he saw, it was truly a wonder and his heart thumped with excitement.

Giorgio saw the young man's expression and smiled to himself.

From his vantage point on the hill, Christos could see the city had in parts a wall surrounding it, with tall rectangular towers with flags of varying designs fluttering from their tops. There was no wall where the buildings hugged the edges of the sea, which itself cut into the city in mirrored serpentine ribbons of water, coloured pink and gold by the setting sun. These, in turn, were crossed and spanned by a multitude of bridges mostly wooden but some also of stone.

The last hour's journey was through marshy land which was on either side of the road leading into the city. Christos was mostly silent, awestruck, the people, carts, and carriages going to and fro had increased enormously, but he only had eyes for the view ahead.

The cart entered the city through a large arched stone gate. Giorgio paused briefly to give a man, waiting in the lengthening shadow of its frame, a coin from his pocket. Then with deft skill he manoeuvred his horses and cart, carrying the precious earth through narrows streets turning one way then another. Through small squares and over bridges they went, and on all sides the buildings, some grand, some plain, seemed to tower above them. Then at last, with night settling in, they came to a halt in a cobbled courtyard.

The courtyard was surrounded on all sides by three-story buildings. The ground floor either shops or storerooms, most of which were already closed up for the day.

A man crossed the cobbles from an alley in the far corner pushing a trolley with a sack on it. As he disappeared into the darkness of a storeroom, he shouted a greeting to Giorgio who called back.

Christos started to thank and say goodbye to Giorgio for his help and company but before he could finish Giorgio interrupted.

"Christos my young friend, I have to speak with that man and conclude some business with him, so come back here in an hour. After all, you have nowhere else to go tonight."

Christos said he would return in an hour.

As he walked across the cobbles to the alleyway, he looked up and saw that on all sides above him, lights were flickering from the open windows on this warm evening. Figures moved in and out of view across the rectangles of light, and he could hear the calls to eat or to go get something. There was a bustle in the air – he had arrived.

As soon as he entered the alleyway, all light seemed to go, and he was in almost total blackness. The sound of his boots on the flagstones gave him reassurance and gradually his eyes became accustomed to the lack of light.

The alley was narrow, so narrow that he could touch the walls on either side of him with his outstretched arms. It twisted and turned, and he started to feel lost even though he had not gone very far. Giorgio had told him to ask for the square of Saint John of the Cross if he wasn't sure where he was, as nearly everyone knew of it.

Christos kept walking, passing large wooden doors firmly shut against the night, and every now and then, an even darker alleyway than the one he was in.

After some ten minutes or so he entered another square much like the one he had left, except this had a small fountain in its centre. Then he noticed another difference to the one where he had left Giorgio. The houses were not red brick but pale marble, and a story higher.

Through an opening on the far side came light and sounds. Christos hastened his step, and on leaving the square came immediately upon a river's edge. He stopped in his tracks as if hit by a bolt, for there in front of him, on either bank, were the most magnificent buildings he had ever seen.

Tall and grand with pillars, balconies, gold decoration, statues and carvings. All lit by hundreds of lamps and torches whose reflections sprinkled light across the water, on which small craft moved up and downstream, and from bank to bank. He could hear song from the vessels and music from the villas, and elegantly dressed people were talking, laughing and walking about underneath a friendly moon.

He stood there on the stone quayside for a long while, watching, trying to take in all that he was seeing and sensing, but at the same time, he felt invisible to those that passed him. He watched and followed this and that person's movements.

13

He saw a couple opening a door and entering the room inside, seemingly to be swallowed by the light before the door closed behind them. His attention moved to what he thought to be a group of ferrymen pushing each other about in a playful manner. One nearly fell backwards into the water only to be grabbed by the others, accompanied by peals of laughter.

He heard a bell begin to ring and it brought his promise to Giorgio to return in one hour's time to mind. So he turned away from the water's edge and made his way back into the square behind him, and then into the labyrinth of alleyways.

It seemed much quicker to return to the square than it had to reach the river. Giorgio and the merchant were nowhere to be seen, and a lot of the lights in the rooms above had been put out.

For a moment Christos doubted he was in the right place, then Giorgio's voice rang out, "Christos take the door to your right and come up to the top floor."

The stairs were wooden and rickety but soon Christos had reached the top floor landing. Cooking smells wafted through the air, and the plaster on the walls was speckled and peeling. The door in front of him was open, Giorgio and the merchant sat at a table eating. Christos could see in the kitchen behind them a tall graceful woman with dark hair tied in a bun, washing a saucepan.

As he entered the apartment, she turned and smiled, her eyes were violet but underneath them were dark lines. She was a striking woman, thought Christos, even now in middle age.

"Sit," the merchant said, "have some food."

Before he had answered, the woman was already there with a bowl of what looked like small dumplings in a tomato sauce.

"Giorgio my old friend, has told me of your desire to be an artist and as I supply many of the studios in this city with their pigments and raw materials, I am well placed to assist you in your quest. Tonight you will sleep here as the guest of myself and my wife and then in the morning you will help me with my deliveries. We call on eight artists tomorrow and we will make the visit to Paulo Benidicto the last. He is one of the most respected artists in this city and his work is always in demand. And I also know he is looking for a new assistant, the young man I hope you will replace died in a fight two months ago. Anyway, finish your meal and then my wife will show you where to wash and sleep." And as if as a note of warning, added, "We start before daybreak."

~ Chapter Two ~

The morning was fresh, Christos thanked the merchant's wife and made his way to the courtyard with the two men.

Giorgio was eager to make haste on his long journey back south. He shook Christos' hand, wished him luck and after a final word with the merchant, set off.

The merchant unlocked the storeroom doors and they walked inside. The place smelt musty yet sweet. There were sacks piled on top of each other, crates bound with fibre, shelves filled with small wooden boxes, jars of different sizes and a set of scales suspended by a chain from the wooden beams above.

"These," the merchant said gesturing into the room. "These bundles, boxes, sacks and jars contain all the materials except gold that an artist will require. We have oils, roots, crystals, rocks, powders, earth and clays, soot, mixtures created by alchemy and even insects. They come from near, like the earth our friend Giorgio brought us and from afar, like Egypt, Byzantium, China and the Eastern Isles. I will never visit those lands, but I hear the tales from the sailors about those distant shores and can hold in my hands some of their treasures, like this colour here."

He took a box down from the shelf and showed Christos its contents, dark blue stones. "This is lapis lazuli and it's said to represent friendship and truth, and when it is ground down and mixed with binders and becomes a paint, we give it the name ultramarine. Meaning from beyond the sea, and its value is far greater than that of gold."

Then opening a ledger resting on the bench the merchant lifted a scrap of paper from it and proceeded to gather the items scrawled on it in black ink.

Vermillion the same as last time.

Lead white.

Realgar.

Smalt.

Ultramarine, four ounces no more.

Orpiment.

Lampblack.

And so the list went on.

When everything from the list was on the bench the merchant had Christos measure out what was required of each colour, then wrap all the items separately in hessian and fasten with twine. When this was done for all eight orders, they were either placed in a sack or crate, and a label attached with the artist's name.

Nearing noon, with deliveries ready to go, the merchant and Christos walked back across the cobbled square, up the wooden stairs and sat down to a plate of rice and peas served by the merchant's wife, who smiled but did not speak.

Before the half-hour had passed, they returned to the warehouse and the merchant spoke.

"This city," he said, "above any other in the known world has the best and most complete range of colours an artist could want, due to the fact its boats travel and rule the seas. They bring back from all quarters, not only the raw materials of paint, but foods, spices, silks, and every item that is made or found anywhere. This city is the centre of civilisation."

"I am a lucky man," he continued as if almost talking to himself. "I took over this business from my father who started in a small way, but as the reach and trading power of my place of birth, this city, has expanded so have I. And although I say it myself, I am held in great esteem by those I supply, because they know I never dilute or adulterate what they receive. I value the respect I am given, but remember Christos, a moment's dishonesty can destroy a reputation gained over a lifetime. I also have a partner now, he joined with me some while ago, he is an alchemist. But if you meet him, call him a chemist, that is the title he prefers, it stops some believing he deals in dark forces."

Inside the warehouse, the merchant told Christos to take a hand cart and load it with the orders while the merchant did the same. The pair then set off, laden with the orders, down the alleyways Christos had travelled the night before.

Shortly, they reached the river's edge and walking along its paved bank for some eighty steps they came to an inlet, where tied to a black pole was a boat gently bobbing on the water.

The merchant stepped down into the small craft and Christos handed him the boxes and sacks. With the loading of each new item, the boat sat deeper in the water, and after making the journey back to the warehouse twice more, eventually all the orders were aboard.

The merchant helped Christos into the boat. He hardly had room to put his feet down, and the water was only two hand's length from coming over the sides.

The merchant could see the concern on the face of Christos and laughed. "We will not sink or drown my friend, this boat has always been a good servant, and it has taken greater loads than we have today, so let's proceed."

Christos sat at the front on two sacks, while the merchant punted the boat upstream and under a large white stone bridge, before turning right into a smaller waterway. Then into still smaller waterways that had no embankments, only houses with doors that sat just above the green languid water.

After a while, the merchant brought the boat to a halt and called up to an open window. A young man wearing a red hat and ginger hair poked his head out and then disappeared.

A moment later the wooden door was opened, revealing an empty room with a black and white marble floor. After a brief exchange, six of the heavier sacks were removed from the boat, and the young man gave the merchant a purse and closed the door. The removal of the sacks buoyed the boat.

"That was a sculptor's house." The merchant said, and off they set again.

Throughout the afternoon they delivered their orders. Christos sat mostly silent, partly overwhelmed and partly absorbing his new home. Noting the varying bridges they passed under, the flaking plaster and patina on the buildings, the odd square glimpsed when there was a gap between the buildings and the people with their multitude of varied costumes.

Around late afternoon they arrived at the last of the places they had to visit, outwardly not much different from any of the others, tucked away down a labyrinth of waterways.

The merchant tied the boat to an iron ring fixed into the wall and called out. The door was opened by a well-built stocky young man with close-cropped hair and three days growth of beard. The merchant said he wanted to see Paulo, and the man gestured with his head to follow him. "He cannot speak," the merchant quietly said to Christos. "His name is Stuardo."

They followed Stuardo into an almost empty room, up a stone staircase and into a studio on the first floor.

The ceiling was high and the room spacious. To their right was a large canvas on which two people were working, one sitting on a three-legged stool painting grasses and foliage and the other standing on boards supported by trestles, painting feathers on an angel's wing. In front of them, two rectangular windows flooded the room with light and to the left against the wall, a long table was covered with brushes, colours in pots, rags, rolls of papers, and a plate of uneaten food. Between the end of the table and the windows were two doors, both open. Centrally and with the two windows behind was a small painting of a man looking sideways out of the picture; his hair and hat in brilliant blue, were still unfinished.

From the door nearest to them, raised voices could be heard. Then a fat man in a black and white striped shirt and green trousers that fitted too tightly, entered the room still talking to someone behind him.

"Argh," the man cried when he saw the merchant.

"Good to see you, Paulo," the merchant replied.

Then after a brief exchange of words, the merchant introduced Christos and told of why Christos was with him.

"Let us see your drawings then, young man."

He briefly studied them. Then tossing them onto the long table, he said, "They are fine, I will take you on. I was just going to eat, will you both join me?"

And without waiting for a response, he called to Stuardo to bring two more plates of fish and eggs.

During the meal, Paulo explained Christos' apprenticeship would last perhaps eight years, but he would learn everything in that time there was to know about painting.

"I will also give you a place to sleep," Paulo said between mouthfuls. "Two meals a day, and a few coins every week to spend how you choose."

The two artists who had been working on the large canvas had stopped and joined them to eat as well.

"This is Jacomo and Arcolano, and Stuardo you have already met."

Christos nodded in their directions.

After the meal, the merchant departed through the door leading onto the waterway and headed back to his home in the square of Saint John. Meanwhile, Christos was shown by Stuardo through the second of the doors, up two flights of stairs to an attic space that they would share.

As he went to sleep that night in his new home, Christos thought, it was all going so easily. Everything had fallen into place without any effort, kind and generous people had helped every step of the way and luck seemed to be on his side.

The following morning, Stuardo who was already dressed, roused Christos, and then he bought his thumb and forefingers to his mouth indicating eating and left the room. Christos quickly put on some clothes and went downstairs to where he could hear the others having breakfast.

"Good morning," Paulo said. "Try and be earlier tomorrow. It will be helpful for our lovely maid Angelica," who was already putting a plate, knife and spoon in front of him, "as she has to get to the market, and for me also, as we have a lot to do."

The breakfast was simple, bread, cheese, cold meat, and stewed apricots.

"Today, Christos," Paulo said while they were eating. "Stuardo will show you how to make paint from the earth I received yesterday, but first, could you help Angelica to clear away this meal?"

Having returned to the studio, the two assistants were already at work continuing on the large canvas. Paulo was looking at the portrait in front of the window, and Stuardo was at the long table now cleared of the breakfast things and he beckoned to Christos to watch him.

In a mortar was some yellowish earth that Christos learnt later had already been washed and dried. Stuardo ground it down with a pestle till it became finer and finer, then the contents were mixed slowly with oil until it became paint. It was then put into a glass jar, labelled, and the jar placed on a shelf in a small room next to where they had eaten.

Jars filled the shelves, and the colours ran the entire spectrum, plus whites, blacks and browns. Stuardo motioned for Christos to have a go and for the rest of the morning, he did nothing else.

After a short break around noon when the maid had brought in some soup, Christos was given a new task.

Stuardo sprinkled a small amount of green powder from one of the glass jars from the storeroom onto a marble slab, and then from a dark brown earthenware pitcher, he poured a tiny amount of walnut oil into a well in the middle of the powder. Then with a flat-bottomed tool a little like the pestle, he gently worked the mixture around and around, adding more oil as he went until it finally became paint. Then with a flexible knife, he scooped it up and put it into a glass jar and pushed a cork firmly in the top. And as before, placed it in the storeroom with a label on a shelf next to slightly different greens.

That was Christos' work for the rest of the day, making more green, some red and a little yellow.

The following day was similar with Christos grinding dried earth under Stuardo's instruction.

The studio was in good spirits with Paulo and his two assistants singing local songs, and the morning passed quickly.

Around eleven-thirty Paulo told Stuardo to fetch two bottles of good wine and ask the maid to bring the best glasses, a plate of soft-boiled crabs, pears, walnuts, and some bread.

This all done, and in place on the end of the long table on which Christos had been working, Stuardo indicated for Christos to follow him downstairs where he opened the doors to the waterway and after looking out, stepped back a pace and waited.

At noon, the bells of the city started to ring out, and as they did, a beautiful sleek black boat with gold curlicues painted on its side pulled alongside the open doorway.

At either end of the boat were liveried servants with their oars held vertically, and in its centre was a rectangular cabin covered in maroon material.

Then a flap in the material opened and with an effortless bound, a man stepped out of the boat and into the room where the two were waiting.

Stuardo bowed and Christos followed suit, and without a backwards glance, the man ascended the stairs and entered the studio.

"Good morning, sir," Paulo said. "I hope you are in good health."

"As always," the man replied. "Now let me see how my portrait is progressing."

And the pair walked over to the picture.

"I see the hat is all but finished,"

"Yes, sir," replied Paulo. "Today's sitting should be the last, but would you care to eat before we begin?"

"Good idea," the man replied, "And I see you have one of my favourites, soft boiled crab."

Stuardo served the man and his master, Paulo

"Who is your new addition, Paulo?"

23

"Excuse me, sir, this is Christos, he joined us on good recommendation this week."

"Pleased to meet you, Christos, I am the Duke of Castello. I will tell you now, you are very fortunate to have found employment here in the studio of Paulo Benidicto. He is a fine artist and a good man. You must have an angel looking over you. Now I would be grateful if you could all leave us as I wish to speak privately to your master, while he finishes this picture of me."

The two assistants, Stuardo and Christos left and took the remainder of the afternoon off.

Every day that went by Christos learned something new about being an artist. He learnt about colour and where it came from, and what the pigments could be mixed with. He learnt sketching, drawing and the making and transferring of cartoons, varnishing, sizing, and preparing the support whether canvas or a wooden panel. He learnt also how to paint in wet plaster, as the studio did for six months when they worked in a nearby church creating a fresco depicting good conquering evil. He learnt perspective and foreshortening, sacred geometry and mathematics, and how to use gold leaf and many other skills.

Christos, of course, had to do many menial tasks as well. Sweeping up, cleaning, preparing meals when the maid wasn't around, and going to the market to get whatever foods were needed.

This was a task which he greatly enjoyed. To wander amongst the different stalls with their fruits and vegetables laid out in rows, or choosing a chicken, some fish or some meat. He got to know the people who worked there, and they got to know him. The bread he always bought from the same old lady; her name was Antonina.

She seemed frail but, in all weathers, sold the bread her husband had baked. By mid-morning, when Christos visited the market the baker would be asleep and Antonina would be selling the bread. Antonina knew he was training under Master Benidicto and always asked what he had been doing that morning. And after talking with her, no matter how he had been feeling, he always felt better.

The market was a windy and blustery place. The breeze always seemed to be there except on the stillest of summer days. With the stall holders calling out, trying to get the passers-by to take their produce, and the general bustle of people as they jostled to get what they wanted for their evening meals, the market had an energy hard to find anywhere else.

Christos had got all he had been sent for that day, except the bread which he always left to last so that he would not feel hurried when speaking to his friend Antonina.

Her stall was some twenty paces or so ahead of him, but as he drew nearer, he could see over the heads of the crowd a flurry of activity. Two young men had distracted Antonina, one pretending to choose bread, while the second broke the strap of the leather money bag from around her waist. And now they were running towards him.

As they approached him, running at full tilt, he feigned to move aside as they neared him but then with a swift movement, he swung the chicken he had just bought hitting the first smack in the face causing him to lose balance. He stepped on a rotten apple and skidded into a flower stall, sending the blooms everywhere, where he was quickly pinned to the ground by the other stallholders.

The second man following close behind carrying the money bag, tried to take a different route of escape when he saw his accomplice sent sprawling across the floor, but he failed to see Christos stick out his leg and it sent him crashing to the ground. He too was held down by the men of the market.

The people around praised Christos as the two thieves were led away. The money, by luck, had not spilt from the bag which Christos picked up as Antonina made her way through the crowd and flung her arms around him in gratitude.

"I will never forget this. Your actions today have hastened me to bring forward something I have been thinking of since I first met you. You see I have something to give you, so be here tomorrow, my brave friend."

Christos returned to the studio later than he should have done with the dented chicken and the other food, expecting to be in trouble from Paulo, but the news of his exploits had already reached them and instead of a telling off he received a round of applause.

The following day arrived, and Christos got on with his work and only towards mid-morning did he remember what Antonina had said about a gift. He thought maybe some free bread or possibly a cake might come his way.

Shortly before the noon hour, Christos set off again to the market, across three little bridges, through a small enclosed square, and past the church of Saint Bosco. Then at the market, he followed the usual routine leaving the bread till last.

Antonina greeted him with a smile and from underneath her stall, she handed Christos a package wrapped in yellowing canvas.

"Take this," she said." I am in the winter of my life, and you are the right person to have what is inside here. My father who was a sailor brought it back from one of his travels. I don't know where that was, all he said was that the night sky was bluer, and the stars brighter than he had ever seen. Take it and open it when you are on your own this evening."

Christos returned to the studio, put the food in the kitchen and took the package to his room, pushing it under his bed. Then he returned downstairs to prepare the midday meal.

The afternoon passed slowly with his thoughts on the package and what was in it. Around six they all stopped what they were doing and he and Stuardo went to their top floor room.

Luckily Stuardo was going to a puppet show that evening that had arrived in the city from an island in the far south. When he had gone, Christos pulled out the package from under his bed, sat down and unwrapped it.

There on his lap was a bundle of heavy cloth the same colour as that made from lapis lazuli, namely ultramarine. It had obviously been folded up in the package for some time but when he held it at arm's length and let it fall to the floor, he realised what it was he was holding: it was a cloak as long as he was tall.

Taken aback, he looked at it for some time trying to understand what he had been given. He felt stunned, his mind gave him no words. He held it away from himself and saw that it was beautiful. The chest area of the cloak had been stitched all over with small coloured beads in the shapes of yellow moons, orange suns, silver stars, and strange symbols, lines and numbers that looked as if they belonged to some ancient alphabet. Christos did not understand what they meant; all he knew was that it was a garment he had never seen the like of before. And he sat on his bed holding it.

It was sometime later that Stuardo returned from his evening out to find Christos sound asleep covered by the cloak. He looked at it admiringly but was tired himself and went to sleep.

~ Chapter Three ~

Christos woke first feeling refreshed. The day was bright and sunny. He made his bed and folded his cloak into a square, placing it neatly on top of the covers just as Stuardo was coming around from his slumbers. He groaned and pointed to his stomach, gesturing for a drink. Christos guessed that his friend had overindulged the night before and went and made a mug of fennel tea. Stuardo gave a weak smile in thanks and settled back into his pillows while Christos returned to the kitchen for breakfast.

Paulo, Jacomo, and Arcolano were sitting around the table talking of the day's plans. Angelica the maid who was seldom here at this early hour was cooking eggs and she greeted Christos with a smile.

"Where's Stuardo?" Paulo asked.

"I fear he is not well; he possibly had a little too much to drink last night. I've made him some tea, but he's in bed groaning."

The others laughed.

"That's a shame," Paulo said. "Because today he was going to help me deliver the duke's portrait while these two scallywags did some work. Never mind you can come with me instead."

From the studio, Christos carefully carried the heavily wrapped portrait down the stairs, through the ground floor and into Paulo's boat. Once it was secured Paulo and Christos set off for the other side of the city. Christos rowing while Paulo gave directions, talked about everything and called out to people he knew on the banks as they passed by.

After the best part of an hour had expired, they reached the region of the duke's palace. The waterways here were wide and the swell of the open sea could be felt on their small craft. The ocean was just beyond the cluster of islets that were scattered across the sea-bound entrance to the city. The villas on either bank were grand and as imposing as could be, but there on the left bank, was a building that was more than a villa, it was a palace. It was twice as wide as all the others and with the afternoon sun reflecting off the water, it shone with sparkling reflections on its white marble facade.

The main door was between two pillars reached by a flight of steps from the water. As the two of them endeavoured to secure their vessel, liveried footmen came to their assistance. Christos and the footmen followed Paulo up the steps and through the dark oak doors carefully carrying the painting. They entered a spacious anteroom with a painted domed ceiling upon which angels and cherubs flew, while at its centre a god of the sea was pouring jewels and coins at the feet of a young woman. There a more senior servant was waiting and took them up a flight of wide marble stairs where ahead of them the sound of music became louder. As they reached the top, they entered a reception room that Christos could never have imagined.

It was vast, with wooden panelled walls hung with large paintings, chandeliers suspended from the gold and white ceiling. And in the centre of the room, some forty steps ahead of them, a group of musicians with mandolins, violas, and pipes were playing fast intricate music to a small group of people. The duke saw them enter and immediately rose and came towards them.

"Master Benidicto how wonderful to see you again and I see your assistant Christos has my painting."

Christos was flattered the duke had remembered his name.

"Antonio please continue playing," he said to the leader of the musicians and ushered Paulo and Christos into a side room where an easel had been set up in readiness.

"Please unwrap it quickly, Paulo, it has been a while since I last saw it in your studio."

Once on the easel, the duke on seeing the portrait clapped his hands in joy; and throwing his arm around Paulo spoke directly to Christos.

"Your master is a genius, you are a very fortunate young man to have been taken under his wing, work hard, be diligent, and with the favours of the gods, one day you too might paint such a picture."

A while later the pair made their return journey, neither spoke much but both enjoyed their own thoughts on the day.

Life continued in its same pattern, Christos woke every morning eager to continue his learning under the guidance of Paulo, and his tasks now were becoming more challenging. He was given small areas of pictures to paint alongside Jacomo and Arcolano, pieces of sky, or distant landscapes which often were drawn from his memories of home, and his ability was being quietly noted by the studio. Before noon most days, he still went to the market, but he noticed Antonina, whose smile always warmed his heart, was becoming frailer.

The afternoons were again spent painting or drawing, and in the evenings Christos would either walk through the labyrinthine streets and alleys or spend a couple of hours at an inn. Or sometimes try the new drink, coffee, at Florian's, a good friend of Paulo's. He would then return to his room at the top of the house, cover himself with the cloak and sleep and dream, good dreams, strange dreams, magical dreams, but always wake refreshed the following day.

Work in Paulo's studio was never-ending, they were always inundated with paintings to do. But they always completed their commissions on time, which pleased their clients whether they be the church, rich merchants, or nobility; and none were more noble or prestigious than the Duke of Castello. So, when he requested Paulo to paint a picture for his bedchamber there was great excitement.

Jacomo and Arcolano could not assist as they were only halfway through a massive depiction of a sea battle the city had won over a troublesome nation far to the east that had wanted to block its trading routes. So Christos was told by Paulo that he would be his sole assistant. Stuardo was a little hurt, being a more senior member of the studio, but understood that his talents had already been surpassed by the newcomer.

The brief for the painting arrived, delivered by one of the duke's servants. It was to be of Achilles and Chiron and painted on canvas, and into the frame would be written the following.

Pride rises up in me and draws me on. But I have learned to curb my grief in adversity, and my joy in triumph.

Mortals who have learned this can hope to live by reason.

There are moments when it is good not to be too wise, but there are times too when taking thought is useful.

I was brought up in the house of Chiron, the most righteous of men, and he taught me to act from a simple heart.

With the studio organised, Paulo set to work. And after a few days, he had done the initial drawings which Christos transferred to the canvas. Chiron would be flying through the air with Achilles riding on his back. Both were taking aim at an unknown target, their bows drawn, arrows ready to fly. All set against a pale ultramarine sky, its colour broken by fluffy, creamy white cumulus clouds, from behind which two chubby angels watched with curiosity.

Paulo worked quickly and soon the painting was taking shape. The duke wanted the painting ready in time for the winter solstice which was when he gave a spectacular party. With autumn underway, there was precious little time to waste and so the pair worked from first light till dusk.

With the underpainting almost done, the picture was well on schedule. Then while having lunch one rainy Thursday, the five of them heard the bell ring at the door on the waterfront. No one was expected, but Stuardo went downstairs to see who it was. There, damp but excited, was the duke.

"Good afternoon, Stuardo," the duke said. Knowing he would get no reply, he hastened up the stairs, entering the studio above with a flurry of greetings.

"Paulo, I was in this quarter visiting friends, and I wanted to see how my painting was progressing." Without waiting for an answer he went over to the picture, contemplated what had been done and said. "It's wonderful as I knew it would be."

Then almost immediately, he picked up his wet hat from the table and started back down to his waiting boat with Paulo following his patron as quickly as his short legs, weight, and age would allow.

The duke had already stepped aboard his boat as Paulo reached the door but the rain, which was now white in its intensity, had made the stones on the water's edge slippery and it caught Paulo out.

His right leg slid off the edge into thin air, and in the act of falling, he tried in vain to perform some elaborate acrobatic movement so as not to fall into the water and remain on terra firma. But instead, he hit his arm on the quayside on the way down and then his head on the side of the duke's boat before making a sizeable splash and disappearing under the water.

The duke was the first to react, and as Paulo resurfaced, he grabbed a handful of clothing on his back, then his boatmen joined in and hauled the sodden weight aboard and shouted through the open door for the others to help.

Stuardo, Arcolano and the two boatmen carried Paulo upstairs. At the duke's instruction, Jacomo swept the food and plates off the table and they laid Paulo's body upon it.

His eyes were open, but they had a glassy look and Christos saw his lips were bluish, his arm was bleeding and at a strange angle and there was a large swelling on the side of his forehead.

The duke turned Paulo's head to the side and water trickled out of his mouth, then he pressed hard on Paulo's chest, and then again in an attempt to pump out the water he had swallowed.

"Get a mirror, Christos," the duke ordered.

Christos ran to the bathroom to get the mirror they used for shaving.

"Now hold it in front of his mouth." The duke said as he kept the rhythmic pumping on his chest going and more water spilt from Paulo's mouth.

"Well can you see anything?" he asked.

"No, sir, nothing,"

The duke sighed.

Then all at once, the mirror steamed up.

"He's alive, sir!" Christos said.

An audible sigh of relief came from everyone as Paulo's colour started to return, his eyes blinked, and he coughed horridly bringing up more water.

He lifted himself up a fraction from the table saying, "What happened?"

The duke placed a calming hand on his friend's shoulder saying. "It's alright, Paulo you slipped on the wet stones, but you will be fine."

With the immediate panic over, the duke sent a boatman to fetch his personal physician Mondino.

After carefully cutting Paulo's wet clothes off, they gently carried him to bed and gave him herbal tea which the duke administered with great tenderness.

Before the half-hour was up, Mondino arrived, a tall man with bony fingers and a stern face, wearing a green leather cape that swished across the floor leaving droplets of rainwater on the marble flags.

"Lead me to him," he barked at Jacomo, who took him through the studio and up the wooden stairs.

"Good evening, sir, it's a foul one," he said to the duke, and without waiting for a reply told them all to leave the room.

Mondino surveyed his patient lying prone on the bed. Overweight, he thought, and the position of his arm was a cause for concern. He knew the patient before him was Master Benidicto of whom he had heard of both from the duke and in general conversation throughout the city.

Mondino called for assistance and Stuardo immediately entered the room. "Go to the apothecary on the Street of Roses with great haste, tell him I sent you and acquire a good amount of comfrey. Here is a coin, bring me the change, and as I said, do not dally."

In the outer room, the duke, as if almost talking to himself, spoke of how Mondino had gained knowledge from both the Arabs and the Jews because for him, learning had no boundaries. He also spoke of his understanding of Greek and Latin, and of his studies in alchemy and herbalism, and how he had for nearly forty years been the physician at the palace.

Paulo went to speak, at which Mondino slowly raised a finger to his lips and gave him an imperceptible smile. The physician called for assistance again, and from those waiting outside the room, Christos was given the nod.

"Fetch me a bottle of your master's favourite drink," the physician said.

Christos quickly brought up from the pantry an aged bottle of blackcurrant wine and a glass.

"Now gently lift his head and help him drink all he wants."

Mondino studied the cut on Paulo's arm, it was not too bad, but he thought it was broken.

Stuardo returned with the comfrey.

"Now get me some boiling water, a bowl, some clean linen, a knife, a fork, salt, and some flour."

Stuardo nodded and placed the herb and the change on a side table.

"Well done," said the physician, softening his tone.

Christos was now administering a third glass of wine to Paulo whose colour was returning to normal, his cheeks even had a slight pinkish glow.

"Now you two pay attention to what I am about to show you because in the days ahead, this is what you will have to do."

Mondino poured some boiling water from the copper kettle into the bowl and cut a patch off the white linen, dipped it in the water and then going over to Paulo gently took his arm and held the hot cloth to the gash.

Although the alcohol had taken the edge off his senses, Paulo twitched and moaned but after a moment he accepted that what the physician was doing was for his own good.

Mondino lifted the now cooling cloth off the wound and examined it. The residue of blood had been removed and the bleeding, although it had not been very much, had now stopped. He then took a goodly pinch of salt and sprinkled it over the cut, again Paulo twitched.

"This will dry out the wound," he told the watching pair.

Returning to the table he cut a band of linen about as wide as his hand and about as long as his arm and wrapped it four or five times tightly over the wound, then tied the ends in a knot.

"Do that every day," he told them both. "And if the cut looks worse or goes green have word sent to me immediately."

Then gently taking hold of Paulo's arm, which still looked to Christos to be at an unnatural angle, he moved it through ninety degrees to his shoulder. Then rotating his hand and arm across his chest and keeping Paulo's upper arm stationary, he slowly moved the lower arm and hand outwards, at which Paulo despite the intake of liquor shouted, but then the pair heard a pop.

"That is done, it was only dislocated," the physician said, and he laid Paulo's arm to rest by his side.

"Now we deal with his head."

Beckoning them both to the side table, Mondino chopped the comfrey into small pieces, placed it in the white bowl and poured a little boiling water over it. Then with the fork, he started mashing the mixture into a pulp, adding a pinch or two of flour to thicken the mixture to a paste. He then cut a rectangular piece of linen and in its centre placed a goodly amount of the paste. Folding the outer fresh linen over it to make a package, he placed it on the palm of his bony hand, took it over to Paulo and placed it carefully on the swelling on his forehead. To hold the poultice firmly in place he wrapped narrow strips of linen around Paulo's head.

"I want you to do this three times a day, using fresh linen every time, till the swelling is gone, do you understand?"

They nodded.

"I have one final thing to do, I need four small hooks, Stuardo can you go and find such things?"

Stuardo quickly found them in the storeroom where the pigments were kept.

Mondino then told him to take a chair and screw the hooks into the ceiling, one above each of the four corners of the bed. While Stuardo was doing that, the physician opened an old leather bag he had brought with him and took out of it a small ebony box. Placing it on the table, he opened its lid and in the guttering candlelight, Christos saw something glint and sparkle.

As Christos took a step nearer, he saw the box contained four coloured spheres, they were red, white, yellow and black and each had a fine gold chain attached to them.

The physician turned and saw Christos' curiosity and again gave that enigmatic smile. "This box and what is in it, is older than this city, it has been passed down through the centuries and I have been deemed worthy to be its present custodian, and one day in the not too distant future, I will be told who to pass it on to."

Christos' thoughts went to the cloak lying across his bed that Antonina had given him.

"But for now, I am the one who exercises its powers and I will use it to aid your master's recovery."

"Stuardo will you hang these four spheres from the hooks so that they hang at the four cardinal points of the bed? First the ruby, this represents spring and air, which will give love and health to your master and render the room here clean of impurities. Next this beautiful heliodor, it is the jewel of the sun, summer, and fire, it will stabilise and relax his heart. Thirdly this black onyx, the stone of the earth. It will repel any melancholy and restore the desire to live in the present when our thoughts may be thinking of the cold days and long nights of winter to come."

Stuardo who was beginning to puff and pant a little from getting up and down from the chair and stretching up to the wooden beams above the bed, looked pleased to see there was only one more sphere to hang.

"Finally," the physician said, ignoring any temporary discomforts of Stuardo's, "This perfect opal, the stone of winter and water, will calm Master Benidicto and restore his visual acuity."

Stuardo replaced the chair against the wall as Mondino waited a moment for calm to return to the room. Then one by one he steadied the sway of each of the spheres in turn.

Paulo had now fallen asleep, but the two assistants silently watched as the physician returned to his bag and took out a small pouch. From this he took pinches of an orange powder that he carefully sprinkled on the floor, making a circle around his patient's bed. Then after uttering some words and drawing with his finger an imaginary shape above his patient that neither of them understood, he stepped back and exhaled, appearing tired.

"We now let him sleep, but till daylight make sure someone is here with him. First though, I think we need refreshment."

The duke, Jacomo and Arcolano, Mondino could tell on entering the studio, had been sitting silently lost in their own thoughts.

"He is resting, sir," the physician said bluntly, addressing the duke. "But he will make a good recovery, I will take a glass of wine after our exertions and then, with your permission, bid you goodnight for there is no more I can do at this time."

"Thank you, my friend," replied the duke.

Then Mondino quickly emptied his glass, gathered his cape and went into the night.

Once the physician had gone, a degree of tension left the room. Mondino had answered the call from the duke and had done his best for Paulo, but his presence had been slightly intimidating, even for the duke. Once he had gone, the five of them, feeling a sense of relief, became slightly more animated after the trials of the last few hours. Although their relief, in no small measure, had been brought about by the physician's skill and wisdom.

The four assistants naturally deferred to the duke who spoke first.

"I am sure we are all quite relieved that Paulo's injuries do not seem too serious, but his accident has caused me, or shall I say us, a problem. You, Jacomo and Arcolano, are barely halfway through the battle scene commissioned by the city's grandees. And they must not be let down as it will reflect badly on my friend sleeping upstairs and your livelihood depends on them paying him. So you must continue at first light with your work. But I also need my painting finished by the close of the year and I am, as you know, this studio's and Master Benidicto's main patron."

The four listened, wondering what was to happen with the duke's painting.

"So, I have a choice to either remove the painting and let another artist and studio finish it or, turning to Christos, to let you, young man complete what your master has begun and that is the decision I have come to. I am going to have trust in your abilities, Christos and give you an opportunity beyond your experience and hope my faith in you is not misplaced. Stuardo, my mute friend, you will in turn care for your master and assist Christos, I trust gentlemen these arrangements make sense and do not displease you. What do you say?"

Arcolano spoke first, "Your plan seems well designed, sir and I am sure I speak for Jacomo as well when I say that the completion of the battle scene for the grandees and the city must be finished without delay for the reasons you have mentioned."

Jacomo nodded his head in agreement but quietly they both felt a sense of injustice at having been overlooked to paint the picture for the duke, but they held their tongues. Stuardo as well as being mute was a little less quick-witted than the other two and had a far more generous heart, and to nurse Paulo back to health and assist Christos made him happy. Christos himself was almost unable to speak, so overcome with elation was he, but he found the words to answer.

"I am honoured with the faith you show in me and I shall strive with every ounce of my being to complete my master's painting to his and your satisfaction."

The duke smiled and said. "Now I must return, it has been a wearisome afternoon but with the help of your good selves and physician Mondino, I think the worst is behind us. I shall, of course, be in daily contact about the progress of Master Benidicto."

Midnight had now passed, and Stuardo having shown the duke to the door told the others with his articulate gestures that the rain had ceased and that the sky was clear with a crescent moon. Also in his nonverbal way, he conveyed he would make up a cot and sleep in Paulo's room so as to be instantly aware of any changes in his condition.

Jacomo and Arcolano bade Christos goodnight and shuffled off to their rooms, muttering to each other as they went.

Christos his mind still reeling from the events of the last few hours, sitting motionless in the shadowy room, suddenly felt tiredness wash over him and with what seemed the very last drop of his energy made his way to the top of the house.

With Stuardo sleeping downstairs, Christos had the attic to himself and with weariness, he pushed off his boots, tossed his clothes onto the floor at the end of the bed and pulled the covers and cloak over himself. Then turning on his side, he brought his legs up, curling into a ball to keep warm against the late autumn air.

Although his body was tired, his mind whirred with thoughts, picturing the morning: he a boy from the countryside with no learning, standing in front of Master Benidicto's painting of Chiron and Achilles, ready to continue the work. And by the end of the year, it would be hanging in the palazzo of the Duke of Castello. And he would have painted it.

Then with his mind calming and sleep about to engulf him, his thoughts went back to the time not so long ago when he would rise at dawn to tend the animals and till the land while dreaming his dream to be an artist. It still puzzled him as to where this desire had sprung from, but now he was a night's sleep from realising it. Tomorrow he would be painting for the most important man, in the most important city in the world.

As his eyes closed, the symbols on his cloak glistened in the light of the new moon.

Chapter Four

The dark clouds of night started to give way to the early morning. The rain had gone, and the blue of the sky lightened with each passing moment, but the air no longer came from the south and the waters around the city were disturbed by a cool breeze.

The news of Paulo's fall had travelled the district, so before daybreak, the maid had left her home and let herself in through the door in the small courtyard at the back of the house. She first fetched wood stored on the ground floor and lit two fires, one in the kitchen and another in the studio. Then with vegetables, half a chicken, beans, and some wine she prepared a soup and hung it in a blackened iron pot over the fire. Once that was simmering, she prepared a fruit drink with mint, honey, and warmed wine primarily for Master Benidicto, and knowing the others in the house had endured a long evening, made a breakfast of sliced boiled potato, beaten eggs and cheese cooked in a wide flat bottomed dish in the now heated oven.

Christos thought he was the first awake. He dressed and washed in the bathroom, studied his face in the mirror and decided not to shave, then smelt cooking and knew that the maid was already at work and so headed to the kitchen.

After relaying the goings-on of the previous night, he took two beakers of the warmed wine and two plates of the egg dish up to Stuardo and Paulo. Stuardo had not undressed from the day before and was bending over Paulo removing the old poultice.

"Good morning," Christos said. "And how is Paulo?" Stuardo half turning smiled in reply as he gently lifted the poultice off, and it was evident the swelling had subsided. Stuardo indicated he would go to the kitchen to prepare a fresh poultice before eating, so Christos pulled a chair from the side of the room and sat at Paulo's bedside.

His master turned towards him, looking tired and much older in the early morning light than Christos had ever seen before.

"What happened?" he said softly. "What has happened to me? I ache all over, my arm hurts and so does my head."

Slowly Christos recounted the events of the afternoon and evening of the day before, including the instructions of the duke. Paulo blinked and nodded his head.

"My friend," he said, "I recall the fall but nothing else and who may I ask are you?"

Christos held his master's hand till Stuardo returned, then giving it a final squeeze stood and left for the kitchen with a heavy heart.

Jacomo and Arcolano were already sitting eating when Christos entered, their greeting was cordial but they all knew the order of the studio had changed forever.

After breakfast, Christos told the maid to send word to the physician about Paulo's condition and to make sure to mention that his memory was not very good.

Christos entered the studio as the eighth bell of the day rang from the nearby church. The fire that Angelica had lit earlier warmed the room but his attention was coldly fixed on the beginnings of the painting on the easel in front of him.

Even after Arcolano, and Jacomo had entered and begun working, his concentration was not disturbed and now that the painting was his to complete, he realised that what was before him was not what he wanted.

Master Benidicto's vision seemed too light, too playful and he knew he had to redraw the whole composition. He worked without pause, firstly he removed the angels, and then he decided to show a point in time when Achilles was receiving instruction from Chiron. He felt the tone of the painting needed to be darker, so creating more contrast, as if to say, here is Achilles stepping out of the darkness of ignorance into the light of wisdom and knowledge.

Then around noon, the physician arrived.

"You sent word that your master's mind may be impaired, so I have brought him a powder whose powers have been known in the Orient for a long time for restoring the workings of the memory. Thanks to our mariners bringing back seeds, the variety of tree that the powder is obtained from now grows here. I will go and see him now to check on his general condition, but make sure you or someone give him a good pinch of this powder mixed with his favourite drink every day."

After a short while, Mondino came back down the stairs and expressed his pleasure at Paulo's condition and without more ado left.

Christos worked and reworked his drawings until he felt a degree of satisfaction and after three days, he transferred the cartoon to the canvas, which was now ready to be under painted.

The days went by, Christos working on his painting, with Arcolano and Jacomo on theirs. While upstairs Stuardo cared for Paulo, whose arm was nearly as good as new and although he still had gaps in what he could recall, Paulo now knew who everyone was, which suggested to Christos that Mondino's powder was working. Paulo had begun to dress himself, go for short walks with Stuardo and spend some time in the studio, though he did not recall that he had started the painting Christos was doing.

Autumn was virtually over, and what trees there were in the city had lost their leaves, while in the houses, fires were lit to keep out the damp and chill, and everyone wore more clothing. The wind blew strongly from the north-east now and winter seemed only days away. At the port, the ships had been stripped of their sails and securely moored, the voyages to distant lands were put aside till the spring, and those still at sea were making haste to return to the safe harbour of their city.

Christos painted almost constantly, and his skill quietened the resentment Arcolano and Jacomo had felt when he was first given the task of completing the duke's painting. The frame with its carved inscriptions was finished ahead of time and delivered by a kindly man Paulo always used, called Zeppe, and two of his assistants. It was a magnificent work of art in itself, the wood was dark oak and the words the duke had wanted, flowed in a harmonious way, interspersed with shells and vines around its four sides.

On the day of the first snowfall, Christos finished the picture and Paulo who had nearly returned to his former self gave a special lunch for those in the studio in celebration. It included three bottles of his best wine that gave a merry feel to the afternoon.

Paulo insisted that Christos sign his own name on the painting and now all that was needed was for the painting to be varnished and the frame fitted.

When that was done, word was sent to the duke that his picture was finished.

The following morning, on the tenth hour, a large barge arrived. There were six crew, the captain and two members of the duke's household staff, all dressed in the Castello livery of dark blue and green stripes. The awnings keeping the deck dry also bore these colours and at the stern and bow, flags fluttered, emblazoned with the Castello insignia, a golden shell in the centre and at each corner a motif, a dancing figure, an owl, a globe and something else Christos could not discern.

Stuardo showed the two men from the household into the studio so they could carry the picture away, but before they did, one of them produced a letter from within his tunic and gave it to Paulo.

It read:

The Duke of Castello requests the pleasure of Master Benidicto and all the members of his studio to a grand festive party on the twenty-first of December commencing at noon.

There were now sixteen days to go till the duke's mid-winter party.

Arcolano and Jacomo were nearing the end of painting their epic sea battle. Some of the grandees from the city council had visited the studio on several occasions to check on the work's progress and to ensure all detail was to their liking. By the New Year, the picture would be delivered.

Stuardo had tended Paulo well and had returned to sleeping in the attic with Christos as Paulo was virtually as good as new. His memory had returned thanks to his continued use of Mondino's powders and the physician no longer had a need to visit.

Angelica the maid was given extra coinage as she now arrived every day.

Winter fully arrived and it was a time of rest; the city dormant. Those in the studio wound down their efforts so as to start the New Year with renewed vigour.

The weather had turned cold, with biting winds bringing snowfall which now lay in mounds where it had been cleared from the alleys, streets, and squares.

Christos liked to walk through the streets, heading to the market. He never found this a chore, and there was still plenty of fish to be bought but the vegetables were scarce now and the fruit more so.

As he walked, fine gentle flakes of snow swirled in the crystal blue sky, and as always, he left the choosing of the bread till last. People dallied less in this weather and passing conversations were shorter, but Antonina despite the cold and her age was still there.

"Good morning Christos," she said with a smile. "I have not seen you for a while."

Christos explained the happenings of the last few months because although Stuardo had bought bread from her every day, being mute he had not been able to express all the detail of what had taken place. Nor did he have the affection for her that Christos had.

When he had finished telling her what had taken place, Antonina did not ask any questions of what he had told her but just smiled saying, "The cloak, do you keep it close to you?"

"It lies across my bed and I sleep under it every night," Christos replied.

"Then all will be well for you."

Christos took the bread and put it in his satchel. Reaching out to the old lady, he gave her a kiss on both cheeks and with a wistfulness he could not reason, held her tight for a few moments as the snowflakes gently fell on their heads.

The falling snow seemed to make the days tick by slowly, and it kept falling giving cold nights and bright days.

Usually around nine every morning, individuals and small groups ventured out to clear the overnight fall that had covered the cleared paths. And in the more populous squares, braziers were lit, their hot coals glowing red through their perforated sides. Atop of them, vendors roasted nuts, or mulled wine.

Christos watched the activity of the city with a quiet eye, and although he had not lived here long, it was home.

The studio had lost any sense of urgency and introspection with the darker days seemed to pervade the atmosphere. Thoughts of those far away or gone forever seemed to be with everyone.

Jacomo and Arcolano were in the final stages of their painting, they knew they were ahead of time and after the New Year, it would take its place in the grand halls of the city building on the allotted day.

Paulo, although recovered, had changed, the verve and vigour he once had, was gone. It was as if he had entered a new age of his life, before the fall he was a robust middle-aged man, now he seemed to be in the first stages of old age.

Stuardo had been given the tasks of refreshing and repairing the house. He whitened the walls of the reception room that led onto the waterway, then replaced some floorboards that showed signs of rot, a common complaint in this city surrounded by water, and put a new glass pane where one had been cracked when a large seabird flew into it earlier in the year. Stuardo was content, and practical work seemed second nature to him.

The maid, Angelica, now that she was with them every day, kept the fires lit and spent more time cooking and being generally attentive to the household needs. She had worked for Master Benidicto since a girl, he had always treated her fairly and she was very fond of him.

Four days before the solstice, physician Mondino visited. He had been in the area he said, and as usual was brisk in his manner, but stayed long enough to consume some sweet wine, a large slice of pigeon pie, and to tell Paulo he was now fully recovered.

~ Chapter Five ~

The twenty-first of December arrived, the day of the solstice party and the five of them waited for the duke's boat to appear.

They had all bathed, shaved, or trimmed beards and hair, and were wearing their best clothes. Stuardo watched from the open doorway for the boat to appear.

There had been no snow in the last two days and the temperature had risen enough for a slight thaw to have taken place, but the northerly winds still blew fiercely.

Standing there in the reception room, Paulo and his apprentices were starting to feel chilly.

Stuardo, standing half in the room and half out on the small quay, suddenly stuck his thumb up and a few moments later the duke's boat pulled alongside.

Other guests had already been collected before them and the boat was quite full.

Christos knew no one, but Master Paulo did and soon became engaged in lively conversation, first with a priest and then a gentleman carrying an ornate sword and his wife, who underneath her fur-trimmed coat wore a pale lemon silk gown. The others on the boat exchanged small talk between themselves as the facades of their city passed by.

Quite soon, they arrived at the duke's palace and although it was only just after noon, on every step leading up to the main door a flaming torch had been lit.

The duke's attendants moved with haste and diligence, assisting the guests into the warmth of the palace from the three boats which were tied up against the steps. While four more waited, bobbing gently mid-stream.

Although he had been here before, Christos was struck anew by the impressive scale of everything. The ceiling was such a distance above him and the length and width of the room were enormous.

It was full of sweet-smelling perfume from the flowers in every alcove and lit with hundreds of candles, transforming the space with their sparkling light that reflected off the windowpanes, mirrors, varnished wooden panels and marble floor. The space seemed almost magical, and at the far end of this magnificent room, on a dais, was a small group of musicians sending exquisite sounds through the air.

When the remaining guests had arrived, and by now there were probably two hundred, a man in a conical gold hat mounted the dais on which the musicians had been playing and announced that everyone should be seated as the banquet was ready to be served.

After the hubbub had died down and everyone had found their correct seat, the duke, sitting at the end, stood and spoke briefly, expressing his pleasure that they were all able to attend this party of light on this the shortest day of the year. Then the musicians resumed their playing but quieter, now with pipes and mandolins.

Christos, seated with his colleagues at the far end, noted the opulence and grandeur of the other guests and his thoughts wandered back to his mother and his simple beginnings.

Before the banquet started, bowls of rosewater were placed in front of each guest to freshen their hands, then the food began to appear.

Small pastries with pine nuts and sugar were the first delight, then marzipan cakes coloured red and yellow, then small sausages and meatballs. Everything served on gold plates.

Next came roasted partridge, followed by calves' heads covered in gold leaf, and then capon. All hunger amongst the assembled by now had gone but the courses continued.

The waiters brought in roasted sheep, it took four of them to carry each large salver and there were eight in total.

Christos noticed that those he assumed were more used to this type of affair only ate a little of each serving and sometimes declined a course altogether.

After the sheep, there were more birds, doves, quail, and lastly chicken, then while the last course was being cleared away the man with the gold hat tapped on the table and announced there would now be a pause of some thirty minutes.

Most of the guests then got up, although some of the older ones stayed in their seats. They gathered in small groups, some stretching, or talking, or briefly going outside to take some air, all the while the music played on.

Then with the sounding of a gong, they retook their seats at the table. Roast pig was next on the menu to arrive, and Christos smiled ironically to himself as there were only four, but then twelve peacocks served to a round of applause as by the cooks' skill and artistry the feathers had been replaced so the birds seemed merely to be sleeping on their platters.

Finally came the desserts, there was custard with a beautiful sweet flavour, then quinces in sugar, tarts with centres of every colour, and lastly candied spices.

Christos felt he never wanted to eat again, although the food had been spectacular.

The duke then stood and spoke again, informing everyone that the entertainments would begin and that they should all feel free to wander his palace.

The musicians left the stage and the man with the gold pointed hat reappeared and spoke, "My gracious kings, lords, princes, princesses, ladies and gentlemen, on behalf of the Duke of Castello, it gives me great pleasure to introduce some of the finest entertainers and actors in the world for your enjoyment."

At that, a side door opened and four figures on stilts entered the room wearing red, yellow, green, and blue costumes, accompanied by two other men in black.

The two men in black lit rings which were about the size of the dinner plates and threw them up to those on the stilts. With gloved hands, they proceeded to throw these flaming discs to each other. At first, they threw two flaming rings between themselves, then four, then so many that it was impossible to count as they flew faster and faster between the quartet. This drew clapping and cheers from the onlookers.

While that was still happening two jugglers in striped costumes entered and walked amongst the seated guests keeping five shining silver daggers seemingly in the air at once.

Christos did not know which way to look when two other figures also dressed in black entered holding short flaming sticks, which with a backward tilt of their heads they proceeded to put into their mouths till they were extinguished. Then on withdrawing the sticks from deep in their throats, they reignited as if by magic. But no matter how often they did it, Christos could not understand how it was done. While the guests were still clapping, the pair each took a sword from an assistant and again with a tilt of their heads slowly slid the blades down their throats till only the hilts were visible.

The clowns followed next, a mixed collection of shapes and sizes, some no taller than a child and some nearly as tall as the doors they had come through. They mingled amongst the guests, doing sleight of hand tricks, like taking a live mouse from behind someone's ear or producing yards of coloured silk from their mouths. Or merely fooling about, as when two short clowns chased each other around the table, with the chaser holding a pail seemingly full of liquid which when he eventually caught up with his quarry, he tossed towards him as if to soak him through. The nearest guests recoiled, to avoid getting wet, only to be the butt of everyone else's laughter when the contents of the pail merely sent rose petals through the air.

The man with the golden hat returned and banged the gong to gain everyone's attention, "Dear guests," he proclaimed. "On behalf of the duke, I hope you have enjoyed this mid-winter party when the sun is a pale and infrequent visitor. We still have two final presentations for your delight, firstly our special friends these wonderful clowns will perform a short play on the theme of the search for love. Which I am sure you will enjoy, and then finally, the duke wishes to share with you something he feels is very special."

The small group of clowns played out a story of a prince's search for love which took him to the four corners of the world before finding his princess. The women were especially moved by the tale and a warm quieter feeling fell over the assembled company after the earlier raucousness.

When the clowns had bowed and departed, two of the duke's liveried men brought an easel onto the stage and then placed a rectangle on it covered in a blue cloth. And with that, the duke himself stepped up onto the stage and said. "Friends, I hope you have all enjoyed your time here this afternoon and evening as I have enjoyed your presence. Before my musicians return and you dance and laugh into the night, which I hope you will, I would like to share with you an exquisite and wondrous painting which has just come into my possession." And with that, he withdrew the silken cloth.

There was silence, probably the first to be heard since everyone had assembled at noon and the duke spoke again, "This painting, as you, my learned friends will surely know, is a masterful depiction of Chiron and Achilles from the studio of Paulo Benidicto. Paulo would you please stand and take a bow. Also your talented assistants."

Paulo stood and bowed, and at the final comment, the four assistants at the far end of the table also rose to their feet.

The duke continued, "I would especially like to congratulate the artist largely responsible for this great artwork. For as some of you may know, my good friend Master Benidicto has had a spell of incapacity, but under his tutelage, a young man called Christos completed the work."

Christos felt the eyes of the room turn towards him and as the applause grew louder, he felt a flush cross his face.

The King of France, the most eminent guest amongst many was the first to respond. "As you say," he said addressing the duke. "You have acquired a painting of such skill and artistry that it rivals anything I hold in any of my palaces, and this, young man –" turning and speaking to Christos, "we have not seen the like of for many a year, you will be a star in the firmament of artistic endeavour forevermore, of that I am sure."

Christos felt elated and humbled by the king's praises, who continued.

"And should you, my dear duke, not find full employment for this genius you have discovered, then I would pay handsomely for his services. So, remember my words, young man when you wish for a change of scene, the palaces of France await."

Paulo, Christos and the others were not staying at the palazzo overnight and they returned in the early hours of the morning by the barge that had earlier delivered them.

They were all slightly drunk, not only on the beverages they had consumed but also from the events of the evening.

Stuardo in his way was just plain happy. He had eaten like never before and with his hands resting on his stomach that pressed tightly against his tunic, he reclined in one of the striped seats, smiling in a satisfied way. As the vessel gently ploughed the blackened waters, where here and there light from a window twinkled, his thoughts were on the tiny bird a clown had found under his felt hat. He was oblivious to the chill of the winter night.

Jacomo and Arcolano had also enjoyed their time at the palazzo. Though without exchanging words, for here in public was not the time or place, they were not for the first time questioning their position in the hierarchy of the studio. Although it niggled at them, they knew that Christos had leapfrogged above them.

Paulo had also had a wonderful time, and the praise his patron in the company of such distinguished guests had given to him made him feel proud. But a melancholic chord also played within him, had he now reached his zenith as an artist? The duke's words in praise of Christos surely meant that his young assistant had now superseded him, not only in acclaim but also in artistic achievement and he felt his light slightly dimmed.

Christos, as they disembarked and stepped inside their home, felt drained by the evening, his emotions had been rearranged with what had gone on.

Having bid goodnight to the others and started up the stairs to his bed in the attic, he knew that not only had his position in the studio changed forever, but that his time had arrived, and the seed that had been planted in his mind all those years ago as a boy was about to flower.

Lying on his back, looking at the stars sprinkled across the winter sky, Christos' eyes slowly closed and the shapes and patterns on his cloak that covered him, glinted in the faint light.

~ Chapter Six ~

The winter days started to pass, the ground thawed and the ships in the harbour readied themselves for journeys to distant ports.

Jacomo and Arcolano completed their painting for the city hall for which Paulo was paid handsomely. The grandees spoke of a second piece to accompany it, so order and balance pervaded the lives of those in the studio.

The city slowly came alive again with the worst of the cold behind them and people now stopped and gathered on the streets again.

There were a few minor commissions for the studio, Christos worked on a lime wood panel, depicting fruit and flowers representing abundance, for a small church the other side of the city, paid for by a grain merchant.

While in expectation of the city agreeing to the second painting, the others worked on sketches and drawings of the sea battle that had taken place some thirty years ago which had never been immortalised.

City hall moved in a very slow and ponderous way, each layer of appointee having to confer and discuss before their agreement was moved up to the next level of bureaucracy for more meetings and discussion. But eventually, they did conclude for the painting to be undertaken and gave their consent for it to go ahead.

Although the city was large and thronged with peoples from all over the world, word of events still spread as if it were a village, so Christos' elevation from being a mere apprentice to a master painter of the highest order had been noted.

While Christos had been finishing the duke's painting, Stuardo had been the one to go to the market but today, due to his overindulgence the night before, Christos went instead. As he walked the alleyways and streets, he sensed deference from passers-by, the slight nod of a head, a half-smile, or the giving of a little more room to pass through the crowds.

A stew was going to be today's main meal, leeks, onions, carrots, some green, black and red beans, pasta, and mutton all cooked in ale. He had all the ingredients but as always, his last stop was to Antonina to get the bread.

As he moved through the crowded market, he could see over the heads of those around him the blue awning that covered her stall but as he got closer, he could not see her, only a young girl with pink cheeks and flaxen hair.

"Good day," Christos said with a smile. "Who are you, may I ask? And where is my friend Antonina on this beautiful day?"

"My name, sir is Catherine and my aunt Antonina, of who you ask after, is no longer of this world. She passed away just before midnight on the evening of the solstice. I believe your name is Christos."

"Yes," he replied, though inside it felt as if he had been hit by an arrow.

"I thought so," the girl said. "My aunt asked me to look out for you. A tall slender man with long dark hair and eyes that seem to look into a person's soul. She told me that when I found you," reaching inside her coat she removed a letter from an inner pocket, "that I should give you this," and she handed it to him.

"Thank you," Christos said quietly, still shaken by the news. With no thought of the bread, he turned for home.

He left the food in the kitchen and without a word to the maid, returned to his room. Sitting down on the edge of his bed, he broke the small red seal, which was in the form of an A superimposed over a star on the folded paper and began to read.

Dear Christos,

I knew my final days were near and I wanted to write down a few words for you, that you may keep or otherwise.

As I told you, I had kept the cloak I gave you for many years before our first encounter, but immediately on seeing and talking with you, I knew it was you I had waited to give it to.

I saw you were a person with a dream that burned inside you. Your every movement and word told me that, and I knew you were the right person to receive the cloak.

My father before his death relayed to me what he himself had been told by those who gave him the cloak: that I would know intuitively who to give it to, and Christos it was you. He was also told that the cloak with its designs and patterns, has the power to unlock doors and transform a life beyond all expectation, neither he nor I really understood but hopefully one day you will.

Finally, at some point, there will be someone who will reveal themselves to you who you should pass the cloak onto.

So goodbye, Christos, till our paths cross again, for it is my belief they surely will.

Antonina

Christos stared at the floor and felt nothing, just emptiness within his heart for the loss of his friend. With tears on his cheeks, he curled up in bed. Pulling the cloak over himself, he lay there thinking until eventually falling asleep.

Spring was now fully here, leaves and buds, birds with songs and pale-coloured flowers waving gently to the bees in the now mild air.

Light had overtaken darkness and the season warmed the faces of the people whose cares no longer seemed so heavy.

The new picture for the city hall had been agreed and Paulo, Jacomo and Arcolano, worked their preliminary sketches onto the canvas. They started painting the sky with a beautiful blue peppered with cumulus clouds, but to what would be the east, there were darker and more threatening clouds which were arriving or perhaps receding.

Christos had not really been asked or consulted on any part of this large-scale piece, but he did not feel slighted. The three of them did not act as if they were excluding him, it just seemed the natural order of things, the new order of things. His skills were not required and theirs were sufficient, so he spent his days in an idle sort of way.

He helped with chores, made paint, although no one pressed him to do so as Stuardo was very capable at such tasks, he talked with the maid about herself and her family or about the lunch she was preparing or walked at an easy pace through the alleys and streets watching the comings and goings of daily life. He also spent time watching the ships leaving for distant lands, but he was content where he was and felt no envy as they disappeared over the horizon to visit exotic places. This city, his city would give him all he required.

Two days later the studio had a visitor, Mondino. He said he had been in the district and called to check if Paulo was still alright. But they all knew his visit was to take a glass of Paulo's wine and sample whatever was for lunch which happened to be thick vegetable soup.

After two bowls of it, some bread, and a third of a glass of wine, he declared Paulo to be in very good health and left in a jovial state.

Their second visitor an hour later was a liveried messenger from the duke who had a message for Christos. The messenger opened the paper and read it aloud, "The duke wishes to see you at ten tomorrow."

The command was short and with a look of slight surprise, Christos told the man he would be there.

The summons had taken no one by surprise and no one passed any comment, but Paulo squeezed Christos' shoulder in passing as if to say that's good.

Christos wandered down to the waterfront door and watched the ripples and reflections on its surface till the working day finished. Then he played chequers with Stuardo till the light faded.

Early the following morning Christos woke and dressed quietly in the clothes he had laid out the night before. Stuardo with whom he still shared a room always slept heavily and apart from snuffling sounds that a pig might make while searching for truffles did not stir.

The wooden stairs creaked on his way down to the kitchen, as they always did, and while boiling water for some mint tea, Christos sliced two pieces of yesterday's bread and spread both with butter from the larder. On the first piece, he had some strong cheese and on the second he spooned on blackcurrant preserve from the last remaining bottle made the year before.

After drinking his tea, he went to the bathroom, splashed cold water on his face, looked at his stubble in the mirror and felt his appearance would not be made greatly better by shaving. Nor he thought, did his appearance seem disrespectful. He then gargled with a diluted wine liquor that had a vinegary undertone and then rubbed a powdered sage and salt mixture on his teeth. Examining himself in the mirror again he pulled his fingers through his hair to remove any semblance of sleep.

Descending to the ground floor, he unlocked the wooden door at the back of the house, stepped into the small courtyard and started the long walk to the Palazzo Castello.

As the early light of the day started to perform its magic of colouring the city once again, Christos knew this was a momentous day in his life. Although he could have travelled by boat through the waterways to the palazzo, walking seemed the right way to go as he wanted to absorb the feel of this, his adopted city. He needed to tread the flagstones of its thousand-year history, to run his fingertips against the ancient brickwork, to smell the smells, the dankness of the algae in the less disturbed waterways, or the freshly baked bread, the roasted coffee in the grander squares or the first meals of the day wafting through windows and doorways. He wanted to hear the calls from the markets as boxes of fish were bought and sold, and to hear the first bells of the day ring from churches great and small. And he wanted to see people starting their new days, local people and foreign people, like the dark-skinned men from southern desserts in their blue robes talking earnestly on a boat that gently rocked while tied up to the quay.

He arrived at the palazzo an hour early, and after showing his invitation to the guards was led into the grand hall where the solstice party had been. Now there was just him, sitting waiting by a side window, feeling small against the scale and grandeur of the room.

He was brought out of his thoughts as he heard the bells across the water ring out the tenth hour, and moments later a door at the far end opened and the duke entered, "Good morning Christos," he said as he crossed the expanse of the floor smiling broadly and holding out his hand.

Christos thought he was going to shake it but instead, the duke wrapped his arm around his shoulder and hugging him, pulled him towards the window where he had just been sitting.

"Do you see, Christos, do you see what is ours?" the duke said pointing at the cathedral across the water whose bells had just rung. "You do not yet understand what I am saying do you, my dear friend? That great church, that temple of the spirit of this city, two years ago suffered a fire destroying almost everything but its walls. Since that fateful evening when flames licked out of its windows and lit the night sky, I have had restored, at my expense, that place of prayer almost entirely and the faithful have now been able to return. But one major part is still to be finished. The ceiling of that great dome was charred and blackened and the wonderful painting that was upon its ceiling removed from our lives, and you, my friend, I am going to entrust to replace it."

Christos half turned to the duke with the look of a child on having received the gift they had desired. He was both surprised and overwhelmed. Trying to gather his words from his whirring mind, he said, "Thank you, sir, this opportunity is greater than anything I could have ever imagined. I am truly honoured that you think I am worthy of such a major project."

"I know you are more than capable, Christos, you have a rare talent that is seen once or maybe twice in a person's lifetime. Other artists of great stature have vied to undertake this work but since the viewing of my picture of Chiron and Achilles no one else came into consideration."

Leading Christos, who was somewhat in shock by the arm, the duke descended the steps into a waiting barge and across the water onto the island that consisted mostly of this magnificent edifice. He strode through its massive carved bronze doors and then stopped at the beginning of the nave and turned to see the look of awe that had overcome his new court artist.

Christos stared transfixed by the sheer scale of the space before him. The pews seemed to stretch ahead almost into infinity, beyond which was a vast altar and above it a golden cross the height of at least five men. Then raising his head upwards, he saw the dome whose apex was so far above him that even standing on the ground he felt dizzy. But what he did see above him was blackness as if charcoal had been drawn across its surface by some huge hand.

"We start tomorrow, Christos," the duke said softly. "And we will achieve a masterpiece together."

The duke's barge took Christos home in the late afternoon and as he entered the studio everyone turned towards him and stopped their work. Paulo spoke first, and although the pangs of knowing his rise as an artist had reached its peak, he bore no bitterness or malice to Christos, the catalyst of that feeling. Rather he thought of the young man as the son he had never had and was proud to be a part of his life.

"Well," Paulo asked, "what happened, what did he want?"

As Christos recalled the day's events, the four of them sat listening intently and even the maid came and stood in the doorway.

When Christos had finished telling of the duke's plans, Paulo declared, "This calls for a celebration, we will all go to that eating place just off the main square and that includes you, Angelica. It is in Smoke Lane and I am told by my clerical friends it serves the best fish in the entire city and that the wine is exceptional."

Over dinner that evening Christos spelt out in greater detail what the duke required.

"The theme is that of the human spirit rising towards light and understanding; and overcoming the demons of the dark that want to trap us in fear and ignorance, so holding mankind back from what he could become. The work will contain battle scenes on a grand scale of man pitted against the devil and his followers. When free of their clutches, man rises figuratively and literally to the apex of the dome to attain freedom from pain and suffering and gain everlasting happiness.

"He also wants me to start composing drawings from tomorrow and as soon, my friends, as you are finished with your current commissions, I would like you all to assist me in every way you can. For the duke wants it completed by the equinox of next year. It will be difficult, but I feel sure with your help we will succeed, and of course, any other assistance we need, the duke will make available."

The evening went well, they all ate and drank a little too much. Jacomo told some bad jokes which made Angelica blush, for which he apologised. Then well after midnight, they all weaved their way back home, arm in arm singing popular songs, out of tune but happy.

They all rose late, and Angelica did not appear till nearly noon, but no one minded, and they made their own breakfasts. Christos was the first to rise, he fried eggs and squeezed orange juice made from the oranges Arcolano had bought home one day in a sack from the docks. There had been suspicion as to how he had come by them, but they were very sweet, and Paulo did not pursue the matter.

Christos started scribbling down ideas for the dome. He recalled all the images he had seen during the short time he had been in the city, and with the addition of his own thoughts, by early afternoon he was surprised by the detail of his conception.

Within a short while and with Paulo's help, they had drawings ready for their creation, so Christos sent word to meet the duke at his earliest convenience.

The messenger returned later that evening with the news that they should meet the following morning and that a boat would collect them.

Paulo felt unsure of his place in the scheme of things but as Christos had asked him to accompany him, he would.

The duke greeted them both warmly upon their arrival and then almost immediately, they took a small craft across the water to the cathedral, rowed with great vigour by four of his men.

Paulo had been inside the cathedral many years before the fire so its scale and grandeur were not a surprise to him. Even so, its dimensions were still daunting and as he viewed the crisscrossed wooden beams and planking that formed the scaffolding that rose to the lower level of the dome, he knew that to complete this undertaking in eighteen months was going to be a mammoth task.

On a trestle table on the floor of the nave, Christos explained their drawings. When he finished, he waited expectantly for the duke's response but there was silence. Christos gave Paulo a slight glance, as if for reassurance, but Paulo pretended not to notice.

Then after what seemed an age, the duke's face broke into a smile and then a grin and he said, "I knew you were the right choice for this work, Christos and with the experience and help of my friend Paulo and his studio, this painting will bring you fame long after my name has faded. Now return to your studio and gather what you need to commence as quickly as you can. Here are five hundred coins, you will receive another nine lots, once every eight weeks as long as the work progresses as it should. Now, gentlemen, I have to leave you as I have a grand council meeting within the hour."

Christos and Paulo walked out onto the cathedral steps and into the bright light. The fresh spring day had a warm salt-laden breeze coming in off the sea, and they stood watching as the duke was taken back to his palace. For their return journey, a single oarsman waited respectfully at the bottom of the steps. Paulo thought deeply but waited for Christos to speak first as they glided past the facades of the buildings along the waterway.

"You know," Christos said as if stepping from a dream. "I hold in my hand more money than my mother and father ever made for all their toil in their entire lives, and I have not really started work yet."

Paulo smiled wryly, "And what are you going to do with it? How are you going to divide it now you hold the purse strings? Remember you will, of course, have materials and other expenses to take from that money but, yes, today you are a man of some means."

"I am not sure how to divide the money," Christos said. "I suppose I will pay Jacomo, Arcolano, and Stuardo, what you paid them and the remainder I will share half and half with you, after all, without you I would have nothing."

Paulo laughed, "No, Christos you are now the master at my studio, although soon people will refer to it as your studio, and I am already comfortable with enough funds to see out my days. No, I will accept twenty out of every hundred coins and that would be generous if you agree."

"If you are happy with that arrangement, Paulo then so be it. After everything is paid, I will give you one coin out of every five." They shook hands which was not only a symbol of their deal but also a sign of power going from the one to the other.

Paulo knew, but Christos only realised later when he reflected on the day, before closing his eyes under the cover of his blue cloak.

~ Chapter Seven ~

Over the next two weeks, as the days warmed into early summer, Christos refined his initial sketches and ferried to and fro from the cathedral obtaining exact measurements for the cartoons he was preparing. All with the help of the geometer of the cathedral Fra Pacioli, a genial intelligent man who with his assistant, Luca a dwarf, looked after every aspect of the fabric of the cathedral.

Fra Pacioli had written papers on many subjects including mathematics, magic and proportion, and was of great assistance; while Luca, despite his lack of height, could traverse easily the scaffolding and with his measuring instruments gave all the detail that Christos, waiting below on the marble floor, needed to know.

The cartoons were completed quite quickly, marked out by Stuardo, while Arcolano and Jacomo were almost finished on their sea battle and Paulo helped everyone.

The first order of colours Christos arranged personally by visiting the merchant and his wife. taking them to eat as a thank you for their previous kindness.

They, of course, had heard of his rise in the world and of the ceiling he was going to paint for the duke. They had passed this news to Giorgio, who had, in turn, told the innkeeper.

With everything now ready and in place to begin the work on the dome, Christos had three days free while waiting for Arcolano and Jacomo to finish their picture because he wanted them all to start together. So with coins in his pocket he went and had new outfits made by the tailors who worked in the alleys near the market, and boots from the cobblers and for good measure a hat by the best milliner in the city.

These men and women worked quickly and on the second evening, two apprentice boys arrived, one with the new outfits and one with the boots. The hat strangely took a further four days.

Arcolano and Jacomo varnished their sea battle scene and now there was nothing left to do but let it dry.

Christos had been given the services of a small craft by the duke with six oarsmen and a captain named Euphemus. An old Greek sailor with a scar running down the side of his face. He had worked for the duke's father since before the duke was born. His family had always been seafarers and he was highly trusted.

On a beautiful summer morning with both the moon and the sun in the sky, they loaded the small craft with the cartoons, paint, brushes and everything else they needed and set off for the cathedral.

Arcolano, Jacomo and Stuardo knew the cathedral but had never been inside it. They too were visibly overwhelmed by its scale and grandeur, but after taking the morning unloading the boat, laying out their materials on the trestle tables, and clambering about on the ladders and scaffolding so as to get a close view of their task ahead, they became accustomed to the surroundings.

Two burly figures entered the main door. "Morning," they called. Their words ringing out in the cavernous interior of the cathedral.

They all turned as the couple walked towards them.

"Morning," they said again, only more quietly and personally this time. "We are the brothers Andreas," They said as they shook everyone's hands.

"I am Sollozzo," said the taller older one.

"And I am Michael," said the younger. "We have been sent by

the duke as we are regarded as the best workers of plaster in the city. Ten days ago we took the liberty of applying the first two coats of under-plaster which are now completely dry. So when you are ready, we can apply the final layer. But maybe for this first day, just a small amount so that if you want you can commence right away."

Christos and the others all agreed, so Michael and Sollozzo knocked up an amount of plaster in metal pails and hoisted it with ropes and pulleys up onto the planked walkway. Within an hour they had prepared an area to work on.

Jacamo and Arcolano followed them up and fixed the first cartoon to the wet plaster with pins. Then a small bag of soot was patted across the entire surface. When they removed the cartoon, it revealed the sooty outlines of the first images, five small devilish creatures pulling a young man and woman into a dark sulphurous cave and the just visible faces of other creatures waiting inside for their arrival.

Stuardo had prepared an array of colours and had put them in sealed jars some days before. These, too, were raised onto the gantry in a wicker basket.

Christos began adding the paint to the drawing, with help from Jacamo and Paulo and by late afternoon the first small section of the many hundreds that would follow was complete and everyone smiled feeling very pleased.

The days followed a regular pattern, early morning they were collected by Euphemus and his crew and taken to the cathedral. Michael and Sollozzo were always already at work when they arrived. Everyone took a break around noon when Euphemus returned, making the short journey across from the palace with his daughter Zona, who brought them their midday meal. She never said a great deal, just laid out their food on one of the trestle tables, smiled, and left again with her father, but Christos always watched her intently.

She had dark, almost black hair and a shapely body and if the situation allowed he would pass the odd word with her about the weather or about how much they enjoyed what she had prepared for them, but her father was always close at hand, watching Christos with his sharp eyes.

Spring was over, six moons had now passed since they began, and the work was proceeding well. A complete three hundred and sixty degrees at the lower level where the dome met the walls had been finished and Michael and Sollozzo kept applying the fresh plaster for Christos and his team. The duke on his frequent visits was pleased with their progress and always left in good humour.

Now that the weather was warmer, Euphemus had stowed away the canopy that the five of them usually sat under. Although Christos had begun not to sit with the others but rather, he stood at the bow of the small vessel, dressed in his new clothes surveying passers-by. He wore his new outfit to and from the cathedral, where he changed into his paint-splattered garments, and if anyone on the embankments looked their way, for the vessel was decked in the duke's colours, then he would give an almost imperceptible nod in their direction as if granting a favour.

Paulo would smile to himself at this behaviour, recalling the nonsense of his own youth. Stuardo didn't notice, or if he did, made no sign of it. Jacamo and Arcolano saw it straight away, however casual Christos made it seem, and were immediately irritated at this show of pride and self-importance. They could do little about it as they were now in his pay, but a degree of rancour grew in them, adding to the feeling of being usurped in favour of this newcomer.

Summer was wonderful, with the days long and full of richness. Christos was doing what he had always wanted, painting; with money and acclaim also his, in abundance. His collection of garments grew, with new shirts, leggings, jerkins, boots, topcoats and hats arriving at his door almost constantly.

The studio did not work on Sundays, so Christos would go to the market with Angelica to purchase the day's food, she carried it in a basket and walked slightly to one side.

He enjoyed these times and believed the rich and rare fabrics he now wore engendered politeness and courtesy, and of course, word had circulated of what he did, who he was, and who he worked for and the merchants and vendors seemed, to him, to give him preferential treatment. And this he enjoyed, although Angelica knew that when she was there alone, on the other six days of the week, everyone was equally friendly and helpful.

As in the past, his last stop was always the bread stall. Catherine was there happily serving customers and greeted him with a warm smile. "Good day, sir how are you, I trust you are well?"

"Yes, thank you," he replied. "As I hope are you."

Then after choosing their bread and some pastries, Christos and Angelica went to leave and had gone but a few paces when Catherine quietly called out. "Look after my aunt's gift, sir," but the breeze took the words from his ears.

Angelica prepared lunch, the main meal of the day, a thick green bean and pea soup with mint and dumplings, followed by pasta with oil, herbs and cheese; then a plate of grilled mullet, finished off with almond pastries bought earlier from the bread stall.

Christos had gained weight in the last few months and his thin frame was now a little fuller, to the extent that some of the leggings he'd had made were now too tight, but he thought it of little consequence.

After eating, the others suggested a walk to visit an old friend of Paulo's who had not been doing too good but Christos declined and went to his room to sleep.

The autumn sea mists had started to roll in and the work on the cathedral dome was going well. They were halfway through their task and word of its emerging magnificence had now spread throughout the city.

People started coming to the cathedral, not to pray but to see for themselves what the talk was about, amongst them a prince from two weeks ride north, and then four cardinals from the capital, all guests of the duke.

Then late one afternoon, the physician Mondino appeared, who also gave his unreserved approval of what he saw. Later, talking to Paulo and Christos over a glass of wine he spoke of his visit to lands in the south and told them of a nasty sickness that had spread through the city he had been in.

"It started as a cold," he said, "then it made the patient so tired that thousands had to take to their beds, and the old and weak never recovered. I have no idea what is causing it, but there are tales that it comes from the deserts of Africa and there seems to be no antidote, only rest, and even that might not be enough, so my friends stay strong and pray it does not arrive here."

When he had gone, they both said how good it had been to see Mondino again but his story had taken the bloom off the day, for if the fever, or whatever it was, arrived, there was very little they could do about it. An hour later their day's work concluded, they all made their way home.

The following morning, all vestiges of summer seemed to have gone, replaced with dampness in the air. The leaves on the few trees there were in the city had lost their brightness and were turning shades of brown. The bustle in the port had disappeared with the large-sailed ships seemingly moving more slowly now they had lost the energy of the sun. The skies were mostly varying shades of grey, and when one saw the odd sunrise it seemed more spectacular than anything that had gone before. With different blues showing from behind clouds of all shapes and sizes, small foreboding black ones, large white ones, and those, though seen only for a short while, streaked with yellows and reds. The collective appearance seemed like a battlefield covered in smoke from gunfire and explosions, and all the clouds seemed unconnected and intent on winning the day.

So on a damp grey morning, Christos had taken up his customary position at the front of the ship when he overheard two of the oarsmen talking to each other.

"So has Euphemus given his consent?" said the sailor on the port side.

"No not yet," replied the sailor on the starboard, "He says it is too soon, he reckons knowing her for only six months is not long enough and we will have to wait at least another six. He tries my patience."

"And how does Zona feel about all this?" said the first sailor.

"Well, not happy but she will not go against his wishes, he's looked after her since she was fourteen, which is when he got that scar down his face. Zona told me he was working for the old duke in the eastern seas around the Kingdom of Cyprus, and she was the daughter of a merchant at one of the ports there when her father got into a dispute with three sailors from the southern coasts over an unpaid bill. They stabbed him to death during the quarrel and were about to carry Zona off back to their lands when Euphemus intervened running two of them through and capturing the third, but during the fight he got his cheek cut open."

"I see," said the sailor, "Well you two will have to bide your time then. After all, Zona has caught many a man's eye and you're very lucky it's you she wants."

The other sailor smiled and nodded, and they went on rowing.

The conversation Christos overheard burned into his entire being, he wanted Zona, could she not see that. He had wanted her since she first brought their food to the cathedral, and he was a better man than this mariner would ever be. Christos seethed with emotions, both jealousy and anger towards the sailor and the desire to make Zona his, come what may.

The boat slowed as they were coming alongside the moorings at the cathedral and the crew made her fast.

"Come on, Christos," Paulo called out. "You are getting soaked, you've been standing in the rain for ten minutes or more, had you not noticed?"

Inside the cathedral, Christos rubbed a towel through his hair and changed into his painting clothes.

The anger was still with him as high above on the scaffolding Michael and Sollozzo were putting a layer of plaster on an area in preparation for the morning's work, unaware of his bad mood.

The colour merchant, after the initial order, was now sending pigment directly to the cathedral, and Stuardo was kept constantly busy keeping up with the demands for paint from those working above.

At midmorning, the merchant arrived and entered the cathedral in his usual amiable way but quite wet because of the pouring rain. Calling up a good day to those on the scaffolding and to Stuardo and Paulo who were preparing the pigments, he exchanged a few words with Paulo and went back to the quayside with Stuardo to start unloading.

The merchant's small boat sat quite low in the water. Covered by a tarpaulin were sacks of different grades of plaster for Michael and Sollozzo, plus an array of fine colours in hessian packages already ground down into powder.

Stuardo did most of the carrying being much younger and stronger but they both got soaked through. The rain was still falling, making the marble of the steps gleam. They had almost finished getting everything inside when, whilst carrying the final two packages, Stuardo slipped and crashed down onto the floor, losing control of the packets. One slid some twenty paces away from him but the other caught the edge of the lock with its large key still in place in the door and it tore the package open. The bag cascaded blue pigment onto the threshold of the nave but mostly it fell outside the door, where very quickly the water on the ground and the falling rain formed the most perfect blue puddles which then slowly turned into tiny rivers that ran down the steps.

Paulo was the first to see the commotion and alerted those above, and he ran as fast as his short old legs would allow towards Stuardo who luckily was already getting to his feet. Everyone arrived within moments and gathered round asking if he was alright, and but for a bruise on his arm he was.

Christos however, paid little attention to Stuardo and glared at the mass of ultramarine lying in pools on the floor. "You incompetent fool," he barked at the still shaken Stuardo. "Do you know what that has cost me? I will take it out of your allowance make no mistake." With that he turned and re-entered the cathedral and with venomous curses climbed the ladders, giving a final nondescript shout before resuming his work.

The group watched Christos in silent disbelief. Never before had they seen this side of him, and to act as he had was totally disproportional with the spilling of some pigment, even if it was ultramarine. They knew he was being paid handsomely and although a loss, to verbally attack his roommate and friend seemed mean and totally wrong.

Gathering up what they could of the dry pigment they then washed away that which had was wet and spoiled.

The merchant made his way home with a changed view of the young man who had so recently arrived from the country and who had seemed so humble and grateful for the help he had been given. He shook his head more than once in disbelief before seeing again his quiet wife with the violet eyes.

The others resumed their various duties but the atmosphere was not good, Michael and Sollozzo did not sing their songs, Jacomo and Arcolano had an even greater feeling of ill will towards Christos, and Paulo, good-natured man that he was, tried to pass the whole thing off as just one of those things that young men go through, but the faith in his former apprentice was dented. Stuardo the central figure in the incident seemed unaffected, but because of his disability, it was hard to be sure.

Euphemus arrived a while later with Zona who laid out lunch as she always did, fresh bread, a roasted chicken, some cheese, pickles, grapes and some wine. They all ate in a muted way and later that afternoon went back home but Christos did not apologise.

~ Chapter Eight ~

The solstice was getting closer and it was only a few days away from the duke's party.

Some of his guests had arrived early, amongst them the King of France who on his second day with the duke along with all his attendants visited the cathedral.

Like all the other people who had seen the dome, the king was extremely impressed and joked with the duke that it was just as well he had secured Christos' services with such a magnificent commission otherwise, he would have whisked him off to Paris.

Turning to Christos he said, "I have seen art all over Europe and employed many artists to work for me throughout my life, but since I first saw your picture of Achilles I have been of the belief that there is no greater living painter and only a few from yesteryear that stand comparison to you. This splendid dome above us, albeit incomplete, will fix your name forever in the firmament of great artists. I know from what the duke has said to me, that we are both humbled in the presence of your undoubted genius, the like of which we will not meet again in our lifetimes."

Even Christos' new-found arrogance was swept away by the king's words and unlike his recent ways, he stood fumbling in his mind for a response to these words of praise from one of the most powerful men in the world. After a moment's pause, he composed himself, bowed slightly and merely said, "Thank you."

As the king and duke departed, the king in his usual cheery way called out to all in general, "See you all in two days at the party."

The day before the banquet the studio took the day off. Christos had ordered a new outfit for the occasion and now stood trying it on, looking at himself in the full-length mirror that had recently arrived from the glassmakers on a nearby island. As he paced back and forth in front of it, he had to admit he looked good, and even the extra weight he now carried somehow gave him more importance.

Paulo didn't feel too good and was not sure he could make it, but after three glasses of apple brandy and plenty of sleep, in the morning, he felt fine and set off just before noon in the duke's barge with the others.

It had been a year like no other, Christos thought as he walked up the marble steps of the Palazzo Castello in the sharp clear air of that late December noon. Again there were lighted torches leading to the main door which would only come into their own once the light on this the shortest day faded, then they would flicker defiantly against the black winter's night.

All the guests from their boat were graciously ushered into the great reception room. They were not the first to arrive as a good number had been staying in the palace with the duke for some days, but the collecting of everyone else from across the city had been well organized and within half an hour, all were assembled.

Christos felt far less intimidated than he had done a year earlier as now he knew a few of the guests by sight and some by name.

A short while later and so interrupting the gentle melee, the man with the golden hat who was holding a small circular gong tapped it lightly twice with a soft mallet. On getting the attention of everyone, he welcomed them all as they were shown to their respective seats by the duke's pages.

Christos despite his rise in stature since last year's banquet had expected to be seated with his fellows as he had been last time, but instead, the page led him towards the top of the table, and he found himself sitting next to the lady accompanying the French king. Paulo and the other three were where they had been seated the year before. Christos after a moment's reflection felt this was where he should be and they, his associates, were in the place they should be, and proceeded to make polite conversation with the young woman on his left.

As the dishes started to arrive, though they were similar to the previous year, Christos enjoyed them more as he now felt he belonged.

On the dais behind the duke, Antonio played the viola supported by a larger group than the year before, with lutes, pipes, mandolins, violins, and a harpsichord, and the music they played was merry and bright.

The dishes came and went and the wine flowed and the talk in the room became louder, then in a momentary pause, while the king related something amusing to his lady, Christos turned to see if Paulo and the others were also having a good time but instead saw at that lower part of the table Zona serving food.

The sight of her transfixed him and only when the lady on his left touched his hand to get his attention to relate the anecdote the king had told her did his senses return to the commotion of the banquet, but now his mind was on Zona and almost involuntarily his gaze kept going her way.

There was an interlude in the banquet and the guests moved around freely. With the wine that had been drunk, inhibitions were mostly gone. Some took the opportunity to get some air and stretch their legs while others talked and laughed in small groups, but Christos just stood to one side and watched Zona clearing and freshening the table with the other servants.

Then as the man with the golden hat banged his gong again for them to all resume their places the king came up beside him and whispered in his ear, "She's very lovely, isn't she?" then moved off to talk with a cardinal.

As the meal went on and the entertainments began, Christos like those around him, drank more and more. There were clowns, jugglers, stilt walkers, fire eaters and dwarfs doing sleight of hand tricks. Then the final act, a troupe of belly dancers from the Indies led by a woman introduced as Badia.

She had a ruby in her navel and danced along the length of the table before returning to take her bow, and because of the ovation she and her troupe received, the man with the golden hat had to bring order by banging his gong repeatedly before the duke could give some closing words to the evening.

Those who were not staying were escorted down the steps to their waiting boats as snowflakes fell softly to be consumed by the flickering torches that lit their way upon the steps.

Christos had assumed he would be returning with the others, but the duke came over, took his arm and told him there was a room put aside for him. He wished him to stay so that they could take breakfast together in the morning.

At a nod from the duke, one of his men came over. "He will show you to your room, my dear friend, and if there is anything you require just ask my man here. Sleep well."

The duke's man led Christos out of the grand hall and down passageways with plastered walls lit by torches. They passed a tapestry and portraits, but Christos was the worse for wear and paid them no notice. Then they went to the next floor via a circular stairway, along another corridor floored with long narrow carpets, turned right and went up creaking wooden steps bowed in the centre from years of use and arrived upon another corridor with four doors.

The man opened the fourth one and showed Christos into his room.

Inside there was a large bed, a small rectangular table with a pitcher of water and a bowl on it, a folded dark blue towel, two chairs their backs against the wall, a window with a curtain pulled across it, and two candles in large brass holders that were the height of a man.

"I shall be on duty in the hallway all night, but before I go is there anything I can get you?" the man asked.

Christos thought a moment and said, "Yes, in half an hour can you have the servant girl Zona bring me some fruit and wine."

"Certainly, sir," replied the page.

In a non-curious way, Christos pulled the curtains aside and looked out into the darkness. He was not certain of his orientation within the palace, not helped by the amount of liquor he had consumed, but seeing a couple of windows dimly lit opposite, he reckoned that he was looking, although he could not see it, at an inner courtyard and let the curtains fall back into place.

On the table was a thin book but he didn't open it. Laying back on the soft bed, with one leg still on the floor he closed his eyes.

The sound of the knocking on the door brought him round. "Come in," he called.

Zona entered with a basket of fruit, a bottle of wine, and a glass. She was tired as it had been a long day.

Staggering to his feet Christos said, "Put the fruit down on the table." As she did so, he moved to the door and turned the key in the lock. Zona turned sharply around sensing there was something wrong as Christos moved towards her.

Gripping her forearms he pulled her towards him. Zona struggled but his strength pushed her backwards onto the bed. As he fell on top of her, she brought her knee up in self-protection against his advances catching him in the groin. With a loud groan, he released his hold on her, and in fright, she raked her nails down his face.

Seizing her opportunity she rolled across the bed and hastily made for the door but in so doing, knocked and sent one of the candlesticks crashing to the floor which alerted the servant in the corridor.

As Zona opened the door and fled, the servant saw Christos sprawled across the bed with a bloody scratch down his cheek. He rushed into the room calling, "Are you alright, sir?"

"Everything is alright," Christos said gaining a degree of composure. "The girl brushed against the candlestick and became frightened when it fell, catching me on the cheek. She's obviously concerned I will have her reprimanded, but it was really nothing and I am fine. Thank you for your attention."

"Very good, sir," the servant replied. "As long as you're alright." With that, he said goodnight and closed the door taking with him his thoughts of what had really happened.

Christos flopped back onto the bed and tried to steady his whirring mind. He believed what he had just said would avoid any problems for him in the morning and touching the drying blood on his face, fell into a drunken sleep.

A knocking woke him and Christos stirred. Opening an eye he did not know where he was, he was still clothed and lain across a bed. He then realized he was in the palace.

"Yes?" he called out.

"The duke requests your pleasure at breakfast in one half-hour sir."

"I will be there," replied Christos.

He slowly swung his feet to the ground and sat up, on feeling the pain in his head, the memories of the night's excesses began to filter through his mind.

Pouring water from the pitcher into the bowl, he splashed his face and it stung. Then the full recall of his behaviour came back to him, sobering him instantly.

A page led him down the passageways and stairs until they came to a small dining room off the main hall.

Christos, it seemed, was the last to arrive. There were thirty or so people already there scattered around the room, a group of six by the window, some couples eating together, and the rest around the main table in an informal and haphazard way.

The king had no jacket on and his shirt was undone revealing his chest. Everyone had a look of disarray, of tousled hair, and clothing unadjusted, and this Christos found reassuring.

"Come sit over here," the duke called out. "Did you rest well?" he asked but before a reply came back, he exclaimed at the deep scratch down Christos' face. "Goodness man, what happened to you?"

Christos retold the story of the fallen candlestick.

"I see" replied the duke in a slightly troubled way.

The king chirped up with, "Some little vixen I wager," but Christos and the duke choose to ignore his remark.

The duke beckoned him to help himself from the dishes laid out on the end table, and then engaged him with questions about the final stages of painting the dome, and if he could expect it to be finished ahead of time.

In the early afternoon, Christos arrived back home and all was quiet. Angelica met him in the kitchen and told him that Jacomo, Arcolano and Stuardo were still asleep, but Paulo was not too well with a slight fever.

With heavy legs, for it had been a long twenty-four hours, he made his way up the stairs and tapped gently on Paolo's door.

"Paulo?" he gently called as he pushed the door wider open, but there was no answer. He went through to his friend who lay not moving in his bed. Christos sat on its edge and took his master's hand in his and again spoke his name.

Paulo slowly opened his eyes and focusing on his young pupil asked for a drink to which Christos nodded.

In the kitchen below, Angelica gave Christos a bowl of broth and some fruit and honey tea. As he made his way back up the stairs, he asked Angelica to locate Mondino and get him here as quickly as possible, but Christos' look told her no matter when he arrived, the healing powers would be in vain.

Back in Paulo's room Christos put an arm around his old master's back and lifting him forward, helped him drink some tea, then spoon-fed him half the bowl of broth, before Paulo let his weight settle back into his cushions.

Christos watched him closely, Paulo's eyes that were until just a few days ago so vibrant, now seemed distant, and the lines and creases on his face seemed etched as if for the last time. He still breathed but he knew there were only, at most, hours left.

A while later a slither of winter sunshine broke through the window, playing its light on the bed covers. Christos looked up and saw a smile on Paulo's lips but he breathed no more. Christos held his friend's hand and offered up a small prayer.

A short while later Mondino arrived. Angelica sobbed uncontrollably, dabbing her eyes on her apron. Christos had woken the others from their slumbers, and they stood mutely near the door trying to comprehend how their master, benefactor, and friend had died so suddenly.

Arcolano and Jacomo said not a word for they could not find any that would express what they felt. Mondino went through the motions, holding a mirror to Paulo's mouth for signs of breathing, and taking his pulse, but they all knew it was to no avail.

The following day Paulo's body was wrapped in a dark blue shroud and laid on an oak plank aboard the duke's boat. The vessel sped along, its sails pulling on the winter winds, to a coordinate someway off land. At that predetermined place, the boat came to rest.

Paulo's studio, his friends and the duke stood on the deck while the red-robed priest from Paulo's local church spoke a few words about the dignity, honesty, and compassion Paulo had always shown to whoever he had met.

With the blessing over, two of the crew tilted the plank and Paulo's body slid into the foaming grey-green sea.

~ Chapter Nine ~

The following morning, the duke's boat arrived at the allotted time and Christos, Jacomo, Arcolano and Stuardo stepped onto its deck for their journey to the cathedral.

There was no Euphemus and the six oarsmen were different, but only Christos gave it any thought. Michael and Sollozzo were, as always, already at work when they arrived but clambered off the scaffolding expressing disbelief and sadness at the sudden demise of Paulo.

As a gesture of reverence, it was decided amongst them all that Paulo's face should replace that of a kindly figure that was banishing a dark cloud from the lower heavens, so making Paulo's memory visible for all time.

Around noon their food arrived, but somewhat to Christos' relief it was not delivered by Zona but a young page. Then as they were preparing to commence work after their break, Euphemus entered the cathedral and with a flick of his head, beckoned Christos towards him.

When they were face to face Euphemus spoke. "I know what you did, and what you tried to do, and if, no matter how important you become, I get to hear you have even looked at my Zona I will slit you open from head to toe and feed your innards to the gulls, do you understand?"

Christos nodded weakly, for he knew there was no bluff in what the scarred old mariner was saying.

"Also do not bother the duke with this matter, he thinks that you just wished for a change of crew and is happy to agree to the requests you make. But remember the passing of time will not lessen what I have told you," and with that he turned and left.

Later Jacomo asked Christos what Euphemus had seemed so earnest about, but Christos just said, "He had got bored of doing the same journey twice a day and he hoped I understood."

Jacomo listened but was not convinced and gave a little shrug.

An hour or two later, Christos had another visitor, a short rotund man with black leggings, a white shirt and a striped cloak, with eyes that protruded from their sockets, so making it seem he could see both left and right at the same time.

Christos was alerted to the man's arrival by a whistle from Stuardo so he descended the various gang walks and ladders until finally he was in front of the visitor, "Yes?" he said wearily, "How can I help you?"

"My name, sir, is Felix Rosa and I am the duke's legal secretary. I have here with me," he said rummaging in a leather satchel, "the titles for the dwelling you preside in, which until his sudden and untimely death was in the name of Paulo Benidicto held in lease from my master the duke, but now he has gone, the duke has decided this title should pass to you.

The ownership of the beautiful house he lived in had not crossed Christos' mind as he had assumed it had belonged to Paulo outright and that he would bequeath it to members of his family, but then he remembered Paulo had no family and only a handful of friends.

Christos looked at this short man, this Felix Rosa with a growing sense of at first disbelief, then of realization that the building all four stories of it, with large rooms, marble floors, fireplaces, a courtyard, red-tiled roof, dark blue wooden shutters, staircases, beds, and all the things in it were now his.

"I am greatly pleased," Christos said.

"First," lawyer Rosa said, "I must read you the terms of your lease. They are not complex and it will only take a short while."

So the two men sat down on a pew and he read. "Number Eight Moon Street is now held in leasehold by Christos Azzurro until the day he dies upon which the property will return to the house of Castello.

"All repairs and the maintenance of the above-named property will be kept in good condition and this will be undertaken by the Castello estate.

"Christos Azzurro will keep one copy of this arrangement and two others will be kept in the estate archives.

"That is all there is to it, it's very simple," said Felix Rosa. "All that is left now is for you to sign all three copies which I will countersign as an agent of the duke and then your home will be yours for the rest of your life."

The signings done, the two men shook hands. Felix Rosa went back to the palace and Christos after putting his copy inside his coat that was draped over a chair, went back up the ladders for a final hour's work before the end of the day.

On the way home, Christos explained to the others who the short man had been and what had now through the duke's favour come his way, and there was silent acceptance.

Ever since the money from the duke had started to arrive, Christos had bought a lot of new clothing so that his small space shared with Stuardo was packed with hardly any room to move. But today and so unexpectedly, he could move everything into Paulo's rooms on the floor below and this he spent the morning doing.

As Paulo had not been the same size or shape as any of them, Christos bundled up his clothing and told Angelica to take them down to the market on Monday morning and sell them, but to get a receipt and he would then give her one tenth of whatever she got.

Christos dumped all his belongings onto the large four poster bed and now with all Paulo's things gone, he was able to survey what was now his.

He now had four rooms. The bedroom had a large bed, two dark wooden chairs with carved legs, a wardrobe large enough to accommodate four or five men standing, a narrow side chest with three drawers with similar carving to the chairs, and a bedside table also in black wood. There were two large windows looking out onto the water below, but unlike the upper rooms the panes of glass were divided into diamond shapes, and some of the diamonds were stained red or green blue or yellow. Across the windows, hanging from ceiling to floor were drapes in a dark red Arabic fabric. The floorboards had been stained black and were covered by carpets from the orient that showed stylised orchards or streams flowing between distant snowy mountains, and on one a magical sea that foamed and frothed; and there were also two gilded oil lamps.

The bathroom was the same size as the one Christos had previously used, but now he didn't have to share it which gave him a feeling of glee. It had a mirror in a gilt frame which gave the room the illusion of being bigger, and the walls had a pale-yellow wash on them.

The two other rooms were smaller than the bedroom, the first was a sitting room with two soft well-worn chairs, bookshelves and a globe which Christos noticed for the first time, why he had not seen it before he did not know. Gently with his fingertips he spun it and as the outlines of the various countries moved beneath his hand, his journey from his home in the countryside to this room went through his mind and how but for Paulo, he would not be here in this place today. He stopped the globe spinning and his thoughts of the past ceased. He looked around, the walls were green and the curtain on the single window was the same as in the bedroom. On a low table between the two chairs was an open book as if just put down. Christos picked up the slim volume entitled *Elliptical Enigmas,* he was intrigued by its title and put it under his arm to read later that evening.

The last room, the study, was roughly rectangular, it had a desk with a chair behind it in the same dark wood with a blue padded seat, there was a single window which overlooked the small courtyard, the walls were a faded cobalt blue and down both sides of the room were shelves full of books. Christos' reading was not very good, but he was determined that eventually he would read every one of them.

Very satisfied with his new living quarters, he returned to the bedroom and hung up his clothes in the wardrobe and packed everything else into the drawers. Then laying back on his new big soft bed with its embroidered cover, he opened the book he had come across and just five minutes later was asleep.

Stuardo sometime later knocked on the door, woke Christos and by gesture told him dinner was ready and being served downstairs.

The others were already there. Jacamo smiled, making a comment that now Christos had the rooms that his status warranted but the others ignored the remark.

Angelica served the stew and sat down with the other four. Before they began eating Christos tapped his spoon gently on the table and told them that earlier he had glanced through one of Paulo's books and would like to read something he had written:

"I looked up and saw your smile.
Then all my doubts and fears left me,
And now your look travels with me
Every mile."

The winter had been milder than the previous one with more rain and less freezing temperatures and everyone was thankful for that.

The dome was nearing completion with three quarters of it now done. At the end of the third week of February, the duke visited the cathedral with some friends and his son, saying his choice of Christos was confirmed yet again. For no one who stood there in the nave of that mighty church had not been impressed. With the work almost finished, the grand design that he and Christos had shared was coming to fruition. Before he left in good spirits, he handed Christos his eighth payment of five hundred coins.

At home that evening, Christos pulled a hessian bag out from one of the drawers and sitting on his bed tipped out its contents and counted over two thousand shiny gold coins. *And I no longer have to pay Paulo*, he thought with a smile. Then he let the coins run through his fingers again until finally he counted them one by one back into the bag and he felt good and slept soundly.

Blossom formed on the long dormant quiet twigs and branches of the trees, and birds arriving from the south filled the air with song.

They had all worked on the dome for nearly sixteen months and its completion could now be calculated in days.

The duke seeing everything was going well and that it would be completed before the equinox, started organising the grand ceremony for its blessing by the head of the church.

This will be what defines me, the duke thought happily, to have rebuilt the cathedral after the fire and commissioned the wonderful painting of the dome. Through the years to come my name and that of my family will not be consigned to dust but will live on because of these deeds.

Ahead of time the mammoth task was completed and the duke, some friends and close associates were invited to watch the final brushstroke being applied.

From ground level it was not exactly noticeable what Christos was doing as reaching above his head he put the last brushstroke of cerulean onto the heavenly sky above him but the moment was symbolic, and everyone there clapped both in praise of the artistry of the work but also for what it depicted, and the sound reverberated throughout the building for many minutes.

After a celebratory drink the duke's party left, then Michael and Sollozzo after handshakes and hugs also departed, leaving just the four with the geometra Fra Pacioli and his assistant Luca. They too both expressed their appreciation and said it would take nearly a week for the scaffolders to remove their planks, poles, beams and ladders. Then everything would be swept and cleaned in readiness for the cathedrals blessing.

Back in Moon street, Christos sorted through the requests for commissions that had arrived since they had been working on the dome. There were six wooden panels of fruits and flowers for a merchant the other side of the city that Arcolano could start on, not a great deal of money but still a good profit. Then a painting of the city that Jacamo could do for a wealthy merchant. While Christos himself would start on a resurrection scene for a modest church four streets away which would take maybe a month and a half. As to the other requests of which there were more than a dozen, he would send word that they would be undertaken as soon as possible if that was acceptable, which he knew it would be.

The duke had drawn up his invitation list. Some one thousand people had been invited, from the head of the church and his entourage, to kings, princes, rulers and the law makers of his city and of those nearby cities and towns, plus merchants of note and influence. Some, the most important, would be housed at the palace, others that could not return home on the day would be put up in the many properties that were of his estate. The duke's staff worked tirelessly arranging the food and the quantities that would be required and his friend Antonio would arrange the music and train and instruct the choir.

The day of the summer equinox arrived, the weather was perfect with blue sky, high cirrus cloud and a warm southerly breeze. Christos and his assistants left their house on Moon Street just before ten dressed in their finest clothes and even the slightly scruffy Stuardo looked impressive.

As their boat neared the cathedral, they joined a myriad of other boats, it seemed like a regatta, and the city folk who lined the banks had never seen anything the likes of it before.

At the top of the cathedral steps, a group of pages and attendants asked everyone for their names and they were then guided inside the cool of the building to their allotted seat. As at the banquet, Christos was separated from his companions who were given seats towards the rear, while he was taken to the front row of pews and shown his place three seats in from the aisle. To his left, sat a man and his attractive female companion with blond tresses who nodded and smiled, Christos remembered the man from the banquet and thought he was a prince from a city to the north east, but was not sure. Then the King of France and his wife took their seats next to him.

"Good to see you again, Christos" the king said.

"Your painting of the dome is one of the wonders of the world, my only regret is that the duke found you before I did."

Christos was about to answer when the air was split by the sound of two dozen trumpeters sounding a fanfare announcing the arrival of the head of the church and everyone turned to view his arrival.

He was proceeded by thirty or forty of his ambassadors in scarlet red gowns and black oddly shaped hats. At the front one of them swung a censer perforated with holes that released a smoky incense and flanking him were two pages carrying large banners, one depicting the church's emblems and the other, the banner of the Castello family. The procession slowly walked the length of the aisle, entered the sanctuary and seated themselves in front of the choir.

The Supreme Bishop stood in the pulpit, gave his blessings to the building and all its works and offered it all up to the service of God.

The choir, led by Antonio, then sang and when they had finished the Bishop spoke again giving praise to the duke for his efforts in restoring the cathedral and finally to Christos for his sublime depictions of the testament of the human spirit upon the dome.

The painting of the dome had given Christos immortality, he knew this, the blessing from the church had placed him on the right side of God, and the patronage of the duke had given him fame and fortune.

~ Chapter Ten ~

Moon Street became a place for the well-connected and rich to visit, and the demand for a picture from Christos pushed his prices up. Even though it would often be Jacomo or Arcolano who had mostly painted them.

They often broached the subject of receiving a little more money for their efforts but Christos maintained a hard line, citing the rising costs of materials and reminding them that it was his name that provided what they had.

A new apprentice, Felippe, was taken on to help with the extra work. A slender tall young man with darting black eyes, who knew what needed to be done, having worked at a couple of studios before. He was a good addition now that Paulo was gone and shared the top floor attic with Stuardo.

Christos' new rooms were luxurious but for the first time in his life, no longer did he sleep well. He would wake at three and four in the morning, pull on a gown and pace the floor or just stare out of the window watching the odd lantern shining here or there in the darkness. Then when dawn flickered into life he would go back to his bed, tired and weary and sleep past breakfast, much to the annoyance of the rest of his studio.

The months ticked by, with the painting of altar pieces, floral panels, murals with angels, and a portrait of the duke's son.

When on the day this portrait was delivered to the palace the duke said, "Christos, I have received a request from my friend the King of France that you visit him for six months and paint two pictures, one of him and one of his wife. I do not want you away from here but he is my friend, will you do this for me?"

Christos knew very little of the world outside of the city and a slight sense of unease came over him, but he said, "Of course sir, it is a great honour. I will be delighted to serve you in this manner, when is it planned for?"

"I would like you to leave in four days which should be ample time to organise your studio, prepare your household, and pack what you need. I will send an escort of men with you, the journey should not be too arduous or long, and it will be a great experience for you."

Christos declining the offer of a boat to take him home, walked through the ancient alleys and squares clearing his thoughts for this coming adventure.

By mid-afternoon, Christos had arrived home and assembled the others around the dining table in the studio. Explaining what the duke had arranged, he told them that on Monday he would be leaving for approximately six months to work for the King of France. He also told them what he had planned during his walk home, and what work he would like them to undertake and complete. He thought that they would have more than enough to do until he got back.

From his purse he paid them half their wages in advance counting out the coins on the wooden table and then gave Angelica more coins for food and household expenses all of which he wanted receipts for. He told Jacomo that he was designated as head of the studio and household, and that if any unforeseen problems arose that he should send word to the duke.

There were mixed feelings in the house that afternoon, Angelica was sorry he was leaving, Stuardo always generous of spirit wished him well, Felippe was not concerned either way as he saw his situation simply as employment, and Jacamo and Arcolano were delighted. They felt they would have more freedom with no one looking over the shoulders and a greater degree of latitude in what they had to paint.

Just after dawn on the following Monday there was a knocking at the door that led on to the small courtyard at the back of the house.

Christos was ready and with only Stuardo up and awake to wish him well, his mute friend gave him a hug and signed goodbye.

There were eight horses and six riders waiting as the captain of the duke's men and Christos stepped into Moon Street. The horses seemed impatient, pawing the ground while breathing out steam from their nostrils in the air of the early morning. They were all black with ribbons of green and black woven into their manes. The riders also wore the duke's colours and one carried the Castello standard. Each horse carried saddle bags which were full of provisions, spare clothing, maps, documents and all that was necessary for the journey.

Without really much being said, Christos mounted his horse and the group started off on their six-day ride and rode out of the city.

The riding on that first day was mostly through flat lands and the group made good progress. Unused to being on horse, at the end of the day Christos was quite stiff and sore from the hours in the saddle. They had travelled almost a hundred miles, passing through two ancient cities and as the weather was warm, they made camp at the southern end of a vast lake.

A fire was lit and while there was light, two of the guards went to try and catch fish for supper which they did, bringing back a dozen or so hanging from the poles carried over their shoulders.

The evening was pleasant, the horses rested amongst a clump of trees and sleeping outside, watching the moon slide out from behind clouds took Christos back to the journey he had made from his home in the countryside. It seemed not so long ago.

Day two was another early start, riding slightly north then south towards a vast city nestled in a valley, but rather than ride through it they would skirt its southern edge.

Then while taking a noon break, two of the party, the standard bearer and the captain of the group, detoured into the city to deliver letters from the duke.

After an hour's rest they resumed their journey. All the while the terrain was getting rockier.

Again that evening, they stopped at the edge of a lake, where the trees were less deciduous and conifers were taking their place.

On the morning of day three it had started to drizzle and the track they followed, for now it was no more than that, cut through a steeply wooded pine forest. Its scent filled the damp air, and the riders picked their route carefully up the hillside to avoid the larger stones and boulders.

After an arduous hour with sweat showing on the necks of the horses the view opened up and they arrived at the crest of a hill. Christos was surprised by what he saw.

Across a vast green valley with its patchwork of fields, there rose into the clouds a wall of a mountain stretching across the entire horizon and from this viewpoint it seemed impassable.

One of the escorts saw the consternation on his face and smiled. "Do not worry sir, we know tracks and trails around this mountain range extremely well. Although later in the year when the wind comes from the northeast and the snow falls, it is by any route impassable."

The eight men dismounted, lit a small fire and brewed tea, while cheese, ham and a rather hard bread was produced from one of the bags.

As he ate, Christos looked at the mountain ahead and felt slightly humbled by its scale, which was an unusual feeling for him.

When they had finished their break, the fire was kicked out and they descended into the valley.

Once down on the plain, the horses gathered speed as the mountains got nearer and appeared larger. The road through the fields was at first edged with wheat, then green waving grass specked with poppies, then vines with white grapes. Passing a farmhouse, there were hollyhocks with yellow and crimson flowers pushing their way through the weeds along the stone walls.

They had nearly reached the lower slopes of the mountain and Christos could still see no way through them, but no one else seemed concerned. Then he glimpsed the reflection on water in the distance.

"The water you see is another lake that feeds a river whose course we will follow," said the man who had spoken to him earlier.

The terrain went slightly downhill for a few miles to a lake nestled below the mountains where they rested, but that evening they would stop at an inn.

The inn was wooden with a sharply sloping roof so that when it snowed it would not bring too much weight to bear on the building underneath. As they entered the simple building there appeared to be no guests, only the innkeeper. On seeing the eight men, seven dressed in the striped tunics, he stepped back behind the bar as if for protection.

The captain noted the man's apprehension but soon put him at his ease, telling him they travelled at the behest of the Duke of Castello, and that they required food and shelter for their horses and the same for themselves. They also needed an early breakfast as they would leave just after daybreak.

With that he put down three coins on the bar asking if that would be enough to cover their stay, knowing already that it more than covered all costs and gave the man a good profit.

The innkeeper after bringing beer, cheese, and bread to the tables scuttled off back into the kitchen to prepare dinner. Some while later eight plates of chicken with potatoes and green vegetables in a red wine sauce arrived.

After they had eaten, they took turns, Christos first, to wash in the luxury of hot water in the wooden bathtub on the upper floor.

Day four and the morning light was sharp and clear. At this greater altitude the air had a crispness and the lake stretching west, reflected the pink mountains that almost surrounded them.

After warm bread, soft cheese, fruit, and herb tea and with the horses refreshed and rested, they set off.

They followed the southern edge of the lake for some two hours but because of the rocky nature of the track they travelled, no great speed could be made. But Christos was told the difficult part of their journey was now behind them. As they rode, the air lost its chill and the moon still sat in the pale blue sky seemingly unaware that daytime was now fully here.

The gap in the wall of mountain, which had seemed almost undetectable two hours ago, was when they reached it, almost a mile wide. The lake stretching back to their east now tapered down into a river that flowed with noise and force into a ravine through the mountains that led to a plain some miles below. At the head of this cascade of water they rested a while.

Christos was informed they would take a trail beside the river and after the descent, there would only be two more days of riding through easy terrain to the king's palace.

Once down the ravine and with plenty of daylight left, they reached the fertile lands below and settled for the night in a glade of trees which were soft leaved.

Christos took time to make some drawings of some wildflowers that he had never seen before and as dusk fell, an owl hooted somewhere in the branches above them.

The fifth day and the riding was easy, it was warm but a breeze from the south kept them all cool. They went through small villages and towns and as they passed by, peasants and towns folk nodded or gave a leisurely wave, it was friendly countryside.

In the late afternoon they reached the outskirts of a larger walled town and although the eight riders posed no threat, four guards at the gateway bearing pikes asked their reason for arriving, where upon the captain of the escort produced papers from the duke.

On reading these, the guards led them into a large cobbled courtyard. On dismounting, their horses were taken and stabled, while the men were shown where they could wash, eat and rest for the evening. Christos however was led separately into a central hall.

The hall was dark with all the shutters closed, but chinks of sunlight still played little dances across the wooden floorboards.

As his eyes became accustomed to the lack of light, in the far corner, like a ship coming into view from the fog, sat an old man, composed and with what seemed to Christos a half smile on his lips.

"Excuse me for not rising," spoke the man.

"I am not myself of late, you see time is catching up with me, but I have eagerly anticipated your arrival for some time now."

"How did you know I would stop here?" replied Christos.

"Because the Duke of Castello, or his emissaries always do stop here and I am the king's cousin, Prince Jean Baptiste of Chenôve, but please do not be formal, call me Jean." and from under the folds of his viridian robe he offered his pale hand.

While still gripping Christos' hand he said, "I have told my cousin the king, I am going to delay you a few weeks on your journey to see him and I have his blessing to do so.

Christos was surprised.

Prince Jean continued, "You see I am frail, and my days are growing short, this may well be my last summer. My sight is failing so my physician has advised me to stay out of the sunlight as much as possible to preserve what sight I have left, which is why I spend my time in darkened rooms.

"On receiving word of your visit to the king, I wanted to seize this opportunity to have you paint my portrait. I hope with your renowned skill, you can portray me with a little more vigour than I currently possess.

"For this I will pay you handsomely. I have set aside rooms in the western wing in the hope you will grant me this favour, what do you say?"

"As you know, I was due in Paris in two days," said Christos, "but if the king will not be slighted, as you say, then I will remain here and do my best."

The prince squeezed his hand tighter, although there was hardly any strength to be felt, and they struck the deal.

The following morning, Christos bade goodbye to the captain of his escort, and told him to convey what the Prince of Chenôve had requested with the king's blessing. And that he would return to the duke at the earliest opportunity.

Christos soon became accustomed to his temporary home. He

walked around the town, it was good not to be on a horse, although having gained weight he became tired quickly and before dinner he now needed a rest.

The prince supplied him with an assistant, Philippe. He took note of Christos' requirements, organizing the colours, brushes, the canvas stretched with fine weave linen, and everything else that was needed.

On the third day, at ten in the morning, the prince took his place for the first sitting. Because of the discomfort the light caused him, and Christos needed the light to paint, they agreed to make each session short, of no more than an hour. Between them, they decided the prince would be painted in three-quarter view, with his once sharp eyes looking out at the viewer. Behind him would be his ancient walled town, sitting as it did on the crest of the hill.

Their exchanges during these sittings were often short or even silent, the prince locked in his own world of fading light and introspection, and Christos concentrating on creating the picture.

Then one morning Prince Jean said without any preamble, "As I told you, Christos my sight is failing, and little by little the world is less clear, the light and the colour I once took for granted is less bright, someone or something is saying to me, Jean, you have seen enough, your allotted amount is coming to an end, and sometime soon you will only have memories of the ones you loved and of the world you inhabited.

"If I could have chosen, losing my sense of sight would have been, by a long way, my last sense to lose but all that I have gained in this world is powerless to stop its approach. So I must accept it with grace and prepare as best I can for its arrival.

"You know, Christos my failing sight seems so exactly to correspond to my declining energies and vitality that I sometimes amuse myself with the thought, although the humour is dark, of which will desert me first, my sight or my life, or will the two end at the same moment? Of course death would mean the end of sight and all the senses, but my game excludes that certainty."

Christos rested his brush and listened to the prince's words, which after he had left, still played in his mind, as a pebble thrown into a pond leaves ripples.

Then with an imperceptible shrug he called Philippe to come and clean up.

~ Chapter Eleven ~

Two months later, the portrait was finished; taking so long because of the prince's condition.

With the leaves losing their colour and the summer sun cooled for another year, Christos left for Paris.

The prince had been delighted with the painting. In it, he looked younger by some years, and he told Christos it was not due to vanity that he wanted to be portrayed in that way. Simply the appearance that Christos had rendered was more in keeping with the image he had of himself in his mind.

The prince had supplied an escort of four men for the journey to Paris. They rode two in front and two behind and made good progress, stopping at a friend of the prince's in the late afternoon where they rested for the night.

The following day, the last of a long journey since leaving his home, they arrived in Paris. The escort paid little regard to anyone in their way in the narrow streets and soon they were riding through ornate gates into grounds with fountains and manicured lawns.

After riding down a wide gravel driveway, they were in front of the largest most splendid building Christos had ever seen, with huge glass main doors at its entrance.

Immediately on coming to a halt, a retinue of footmen scurried about, taking the horses to the stables and the riders to their quarters, but Christos, although hot and dusty was taken to see the king.

He was led through rooms with mirrored walls and painted ceilings of great opulence. The attendant knocked briefly on a cream and gold panelled door, and Christos entered.

The king, unaware of their arrival, was laughing uproariously with two women and another man, his wig was across the room on the floor. The four were taking it in turns to hop from one chalk square to another drawn on the floor in the form of a spiral.

The king was still laughing at the finish of his turn when he saw Christos waiting by the door and with a yell of delight shouted, "My friend, you're finally here!"

With a strong arm around his waist, he pulled the tired artist towards his friends and introduced him, while giving him a goblet of wine. He quickly explained the rules of the game they were playing and had Christos hopping backwards and forwards and partying with the rest of them until the early hours, when eventually Christos weaved his way with the help of one of the pages to his rooms where he slept to the following midday.

The king wanted more than his cousin. He wanted a portrait of himself first, then of his companion Isabella, then one of them both and finally, one of him and his court.

This Christos knew, would take much longer than the six months that had been arranged, but the duke had given his blessing to the agreement, so the decision was taken out of his hands.

The king sent word to the duke that Christos might be delayed a little longer than expected, and a note was added from Christos that Jacamo and the others should be kept in work.

Back in Moon street, Jacomo, Arcolano, Stuardo, and Felipe were still working on the commissions they had been left, but the atmosphere in the studio had lightened.

They all started a little later in the morning and if they felt inclined finished earlier. Also the animosity that had been growing between Jacomo and Arcolano towards Christos had lessened, simply because he was not around but they still felt grossly underpaid for what they did and that rankled.

Then one wet afternoon when Felipe was out, Stuardo was sleeping, and Angelica was visiting her family, Jacomo and Arcolano thought they would have a look around Christos' rooms.

Not much seemed to have changed since the days of Paulo, except they were not as tidy, with books and drawings in piles on every flat surface. When they peered into the wardrobes and drawers, they saw that they were packed with clothes which were much finer than Paulo had ever had.

Their curiosity satisfied, they went to leave but as Arcolano moved from the window to the door a floorboard creaked and gave way slightly under his foot. Looking down, there was an oddness to it and Arcolano took a small knife he kept inside the top of his boot and squatted down.

Jacomo asked what he was doing as Arcolano worked around the edges of the floorboard till it lifted and came free, the piece of board was only about a foot in length but looking into the space underneath, Arcolano let out a knowing sigh. "Come and look at this," he said.

He pulled out three green bags, the sound of which told them both they were full of coins. Tipping the bags' contents onto the bed, revealed over three hundred gold and silver coins. They looked at each other with wry smiles.

Jacomo and Arcolano continued their work as normal but with a renewed pleasure, so many of the injustices they had felt since Christos had arrived those years ago seemed to have been washed away.

They thought about what they would do with the money which was enough to keep them in comfort for the rest of their days, and decided to go south to where Arcolano's brother lived. There they would easily get another position in a studio.

For now, they remained in Moon Street, planning to leave when they got word of Christos' return, because while he was away, they were still getting paid.

They also decided to take Stuardo with them as they felt he had been equally badly treated by Christos. Besides he was a good friend who needed their help.

Christos took a long time on the picture of the king as there were numerous days the king did not turn up for sittings, or when he did, he fidgeted and would not sit still.

Also Christos' verve and energy had slowed. Every evening there was music and dancing and the attractions of the ladies of the court, and as he had done for some time, he was eating and drinking to excess. The slim frame he once had was a thing of the past, so going to sleep in the early hours after his nightly reveries was sapping his energy and slowing him down.

Eventually to the king's acclaim, the painting was finished, for which there was a lavish reception to mark its unveiling in the western hall that looked out on the topiary gardens.

Of course, afterwards there was a banquet. There was a speech by the king which culminated in the presentation of a special gold sash to Christos, to which the king pinned a large pearl encrusted brooch, and the assembled courtiers applauded.

On the departure of the king and Christos, the gentlemen bowed and the ladies curtsied and with a newly acquired gesture copied from the king, Christos waved his hand in a gentle circular motion while holding his handkerchief between his fingers in recognition of their appreciation.

At Moon Street, the duke good to his word, kept the studio busy through his wide range of influence. By couriers, the duke was kept informed of what Christos was doing, but like a father awaiting a son's return, he looked forward to seeing his friend and protégé again.

At this time of year, the king usually went south to stay with his friends and allies in Iberia, stopping at various residences before heading northeast along the coast to be with the duke for his mid-winter party. This year, with Christos with him, that had to be cancelled.

Christos painted Isabella, the king's young companion which took him through into the new year. The picture of them both together was finished in the spring, and by the time he had finished the group portraits it was summer, and a year had passed since his arrival. It was time to return home.

A message was sent to the duke telling of Christos' impending return, and it was passed onto Jacamo and Arcolano.

They were in some ways sorry to leave Moon Street, although they knew they had to leave now.

That afternoon they told Stuardo their plan, saying they needed a fresh challenge but not mentioning the money they had stolen. They also stated they had heard that Christos, on his return, would no longer be using their services as he was bringing with him some French assistants that had worked with him in Paris.

Stuardo felt sad about leaving without saying goodbye to his friend, but the two of them had convinced him, added that positions were open for all of them in the south but unless they moved quickly, they would be taken by someone else.

So that night they packed, told the same story to Angelica and Felipe, and just after five the following morning, left Moon Street for the last time.

Christos departed Paris with much ceremony, accompanied by an escort of the king's men.

He was now richer, fatter and older. The journey he had made a year earlier seemed much longer ago than that. Although he gave it no thought, the joy of the simplicity and splendour of nature as he rode home no longer touched him.

The clouds no longer took his thoughts to another place, the green of the leaves and grasses no longer refreshed his eye, the streams as they raced across the rocks and boulders heading for the ocean no longer invigorated him, and the soaring mountains no longer awed him but were merely an obstacle on his path. Even the sight of his city as the party reached a vantage point on a hill, didn't give him the thrill it had those years before.

He entered the house from the door in the courtyard arriving just after the sun had set. The rooms were dark at this hour so he lit a lamp and called out but there was no reply.

He looked about familiarising himself but although a well-appointed house, the rooms now seemed small. Climbing the stairs to the first floor, he entered the studio.

To his left was the large oak table at which so many meals had been eaten and on which he had first ground colours for Paulo. The easel ahead of him was empty and with the shutters beyond it open, the odd twinkle of yellow light revealed itself in the now dark sky. To his right were two panels of fruit and flowers in full abundance, and even in this light, he thought they had been well done but it did not cheer his humour.

Going upstairs, he opened the door to his rooms, pushed off his boots and lay on the bed. Dragging a cover across himself, he closed his eyes.

The following morning sounds from below woke him. Lifting his heavy frame off the bed, he went downstairs.

Angelica let out a small scream when he appeared in the doorway, "Oh excuse me, sir," she said, as she realised who it was. You startled me as I was not expecting you till later tonight or tomorrow."

He gave her a weary smile and said that they had made good progress and so arrived early.

Angelica made him some tea and cut two slices of bread toasting them slightly on the fire. She spread them with butter and honey which had been gathered by an old couple who lived on the hills behind the city.

"It's very good to see you again, sir, after so long, you must have seen some wonderful sights at the French court."

"Yes, it was all something to behold, but I am back now," he said with a note of disappointment.

"May I ask where the assistants are you have brought with you?" she said.

"What assistants? I have no one with me, the king's escort is staying at the palace and will start their return this morning."

"I'm sorry," she said. "It's just that before they left, Jacamo and Arcolano said that you did not need them anymore and that you were bringing new assistants from Paris to replace them. That was their reason for leaving."

Jumping up from the table, Christos demanded when this was, and timidly Angelica told him it was three days ago.

Christos pushed past her, knocking a plate out of her hands which crashed to the floor and went back upstairs to his rooms.

Angelica from the bottom of the stairs could hear frantic sounds as Christos banged about above. Then she heard a desperate cry of rage followed by, "The bastards, the swine, I'll kill them, I'll kill them."

Christos had discovered the floorboard in his bedroom had been lifted and the three bags of coins he had hidden there were gone.

Angelica could not hear anything else. It was silent, for Christos was checking his other hiding places to see if they too had been discovered.

In his study he had a hollowed-out book with various jewels and pearls in it but to his relief, they were still there. Then he went up to his old room in the attic where underneath a heavy chest there were another four bags of coin, both silver and gold, and they hadn't been touched.

After an hour he returned to the kitchen, having been all over the house, and although still shaking with anger, he had found that Jacamo and Arcolano had only taken a small part of his hoarded wealth, and for this, he felt slightly relieved.

"They stole my money Angelica, after all I did for them, and I see Stuardo has left with those curs too. I will track them down and make them pay, mark my words."

"Stuardo did not want to leave that I know, but they told him you had no place for him here anymore, and I'm sure he would not have stolen from you."

He looked down at the table, "You're probably right, I do not blame him, it was the doing of those two dogs."

The atmosphere of nervousness on Angelica's part and barely contained anger on Christos' part was broken by the arrival of Felipe.

"Good morning, you look well," he said, oblivious of the last hour's turmoil. "And if I may say, you seem to be more substantial than you were." He meant fatter but chose his words the right side of that line between bald honesty and amusing observation for himself.

Christos knew exactly what Felipe meant, but his cheek was endearing and diluted his bad mood.

Christos briefly recounted his time in France to Felipe and Angelica and then added, "As those two ungrateful low life assistants have run away, we will need some help here, so can you find someone?"

"I know the very person," Felipe replied, "My younger brother Carlo, he is working for some dauber on the other side of the city, I'll go and get him."

"Good." Addressing them now in a better mood, Christos said, "Now I have to get ready and pay my respects to the duke and give him letters from the king, so I'll see you this afternoon with your brother."

At the palace, the page led Christos through the empty main hall, and knocking on a wooden door at its far end, entered without waiting for a reply.

The duke was sitting with his back to them, facing a window which overlooked a garden. A garden was rare in the city and this one contained fruit trees, shrubs, and flowers.

Hearing the door open, the duke turned his head and on seeing who it was, dropped the book he had been studying on a low table in front of him and rose with a broad smile.

The two sat for some time talking over Christos' visits with the prince and then the king. While they took refreshments, they discussed new projects the duke had in mind.

Sometime later the page again knocked and on entering reminding the duke that the emissary from an African nation was waiting.

The duke shrugged, smiled, and said, "The affairs of state and trade, Christos, they are necessary but consume my time when I would rather be talking to you or studying my books like the one here."

Leafing through a few pages, he showed Christos what he had earlier been looking at, the pages were of symbols above inscriptions and although it was only a glance, they somehow seemed recognisable.

~ Chapter Twelve ~

The months went by and life in Moon Street carried on almost as before. Felipe and his brother were able assistants and Angelica tended to the needs of the household.

Christos though, had become less pleasant, and if something was not to his liking, he went into a rage which made the delicate Angelica nervous. As well as his quick temper, his conceit and vanity grew. Rather than building respect and admiration in those that knew him, they avoided him and laughed mockingly behind his back at the ridiculous figure they now saw him as. But he was oblivious to it all.

Two years later Christos was elected onto the city council. Its number was strictly limited but someone had died and with the influence of the duke backing him, one frosty November morning the robes of office were placed on his shoulders. His role was to oversee and approve or otherwise, anything artistic that was created under the auspices of the city.

This new-found power merely added grist to the now jealous, controlling, and envious side of his character. If he felt his eminence among the artists of the city was threatened by anyone with new inventions, skills, or talent, then Christos would do whatever he could to ensure the artist did not prosper.

The seasons rolled by with continuous production from the studio and coupled with his civic duties and functions, Christos was always busy. His life seemed full of plenty to the onlooker. He escorted numerous attractive women to balls and banquets and though no relationships were formed, he brushed that aside.

Then in the afternoon of a stifling hot day when the sails and flags on the boats in the harbour hung listlessly, and if possible, the people of the city stayed indoors keeping out of the heat, a messenger arrived at the courtyard door.

He was hot and perspiration formed little beads of moisture on his forehead as Angelica greeted him. On showing him indoors, she offered him a drink which he declined, saying he had a paper of great importance to deliver to Master Azzurro.

She led him upstairs, passing the studio where Felipe and his brother were working, and up to the next floor where they found Christos languidly lying on his bed leafing through some sketches.

"This man has an important document for you, master," Angelica said.

The messenger presented it rather awkwardly as Christos stayed lying on the bed. He then bowed and turning to Angelica, she showed him out.

Christos read the letter then slowly placed his legs on the floor.

They felt heavy, weighed down as if with lead weights and a sense of inertia shot through him.

After some time, he stood, feeling the cold reality of life on every side.

Going downstairs, he entered the studio, he spoke to Felipe and his brother, bluntly saying, "The duke is dead. He died this morning."

Turning, he went into the kitchen and sitting down at the table told the same to Angelica. He did not want any reply and none could be given.

Then calling through to Felipe he said, "Summon me a boat I must go to the palace straight away."

Within a few minutes, the boat arrived and Christos set off for the palace with permutations of thoughts clicking and whirring in his mind.

When he arrived, there were already a lot of people there. The bishop of the city with half a dozen of his attendants in their red robes, members of the council talking furtively in little huddles, Mondino the physician sitting on a couch holding the hand of the duke's widow who was crying, Felix Rosa who was pacing back and forth in an agitated way with a book under his arm, Fra Paciolli with Luca shadowing a couple of steps behind, the duke's son, assembled dignitaries and staff of the palace and also Euphemus whose steely look caused Christos a moment of anxiety.

After an hour or so all those except the bishop and his entourage, Mondino, Fra Pacioli, Luca, and the duke's wife and son had departed. Everyone had expressed all the words of consolation they could muster sincere or feigned. Some left in groups, some singularly like Christos, who returned to the oppressive early evening heat with thoughts of the duke's death and its implications filling his mind.

The duke's casket arrived before dark on a vessel draped with black satin swathes along its sides, black sails, and the crew in black uniform.

All the windows in the palace were shuttered and at the far end of the grand hall in the now muted light, the casket was placed on a large table, again covered with black cloth.

Onto this, the duke's closest servants, including Euphemus, laid out his body while the bishop and his attendants said prayers. At each corner of the casket was placed a thick candle that when lit would burn for twenty-four hours and at the head of the casket was placed a large floral display, white chrysanthemums interspersed with fern and boughs of oak.

Word of the duke's death was sent throughout the city, and by horse-backed messengers to places more distant, including the King of France.

It was made known that should anyone wish to pay their last respects they could do so up until his burial in a days' time and sign or make a mark in the book of condolence, or simply say a prayer for the passing of a good man.

As the candles guttered and their lights one by one went out, the time of lying in state came to an end, for the twenty-four hours had now passed. Those still waiting on the palace steps to pay their last respects were kindly told time had run out and turned away.

The same close servants who had aided the bishop in placing the duke in the casket, now themselves said their goodbyes, and some like Euphemus had a tear in their eye as the lid was closed.

The lid was fastened tight, then two wooden poles one on either side were slid through metal rings and six pallbearers lifted the casket onto their shoulders.

The bishop led the procession out of the palace with the duke's widow and son, who was now the new duke, followed by the people who had been there a day earlier, Mondino, Fra Pacioli and Luca, the city council and towards the rear Christos.

The vessel that had delivered the casket now bore it again. It was substantial enough to not only accommodate most of the closest mourners, the bishop and his people, the crew, but also twelve drummers.

The sea was calm, flat as green glass, and the heat, although it was late afternoon, was stifling, even two leagues out to sea.

The captain, at a point determined by distance from the shore, brought the boat to a stop and dropped anchor, and the flotilla of boats that had been following them did the same. Only before they reached a dead stop, they formed a wide circle so that everyone on board every boat could witness the final act.

The pallbearers lifted the coffin onto a flat board at the side of the boat while the bishop said prayers. When that was finished, the twelve drummers commenced a solemn beat and then on an almost imperceptible nod from the new duke, the pallbearers tilted the board and the coffin slid off it, splashing into the water. The drummers stopped and the only sounds Christos could hear were the duke's widow quietly weeping and the sound of a gull flying back towards land.

There was a reception after their return from the burial, Antonio with a small band of musicians played sombre music at the back of the great hall while food of every type lay on long tables.

The new duke and his mother intermingled, passing the odd word or piece of light conversation as they went amongst the guests.

The young duke reached Christos, who expressed his sorrow at the loss of his father and said what so many others before him had said.

The new duke thanked him, then surprisingly, as it was the reception of his father's funeral, the young duke asked him what he thought of a young artist named Veraccio.

Christos who was well aware of him and knowing that he was a precocious talent, shrugged in an attempt to downplay what he truly thought. He answered saying he thought his talents were perhaps above average but he still had a lot to learn.

The new duke listened attentively half-smiling and said. "I think he is extremely good and have decided to commission him to paint a picture of my father's life that I shall hang here in this room. I was hoping you would have thought him worthy of such an undertaking but I do not get that feeling from you."

Christos feeling outmanoeuvred tried subtly to retract what he had inferred, but both men knew the other's viewpoint.

Christos left shortly after the brief conversation with the young duke, deep in thought. The past few days had seen the death of his friend and patron and now his son was about to replace him, or so he felt, with a younger artist.

He asked the boatman to put him ashore a way off from Moon Street for he needed to walk, to feel his steps on the ancient slabs of the paths and alleyways and to move at his pace, as an antidote to the tangle of thoughts that seemed to engulf him.

He watched the night clouds above on that hot evening but even they seemed in confusion with each other as they raced this way and that blown by the southern wind. While the moon itself seemed to be playing games, appearing one moment brightly in a silver glimpse then going into hiding behind a dark cloud the next.

It seemed to foretell the arrival of a storm, which mirrored the sense of unease Christos felt at what appeared to be coming his way.

To calm and bolster his mind he thought of what he had, his well-appointed house, his position within the city, his contacts and influence, his wealth and his reputation across Europe.

But later lying on his bed, the unease returned.

~ Chapter Thirteen ~

The year wound down with everything on the surface seemingly unchanged. Felipe and his brother had enough to do but no commissions came from the new duke, who did get Veraccio to undertake the painting on his father's life.

The decision, though not common knowledge, was known to those on the city council, of which the young duke was now a member.

When attending meetings concerning the city, Christos sensed that little groups and huddles of those he had thought to be friends went silent when he approached.

His opinion on what artistically the city should do was still sought, but he suspected that decisions had already been made on anything important before he got up to speak.

The young duke's protégé, Veraccio, had become the artist the influential and wealthy wanted more and more, not Christos. So nominally his position was the ultimate word on what should be created within the city walls but in reality, his power was gone. No one was going to side against the new duke and his preferences if they had any sense or aspirations.

Throughout the autumn, the humour of Christos matched that of the season. He no longer wore his bright clothes, his colours becoming muted, greys, browns and blacks became his fashion. When walking through the squares, alleys, or marketplaces, he no longer moved with an arrogant stride but instead wanted to meld into the crowd and go about his daily tasks unnoticed.

His invitation for the solstice banquet arrived, as it had for many years from the old duke, and his spirits lifted, rekindling memories of those special evenings at the palace, and especially his second visit when his world was catapulted from being merely an assistant to Paulo to a highly praised artist vaunted by the King of France.

The afternoon of the banquet arrived, Felipe and his brother Carlo were not invited, and Christos boarded the boat to the palace alone.

The weather was cold, with sleet blowing in the air, sticking and freezing into Christos beard as they headed to the palace.

A beard which was now grey. It had grown partly from apathy – no interest in how the world viewed him, but also from the tedium of shaving, there seemed no point. All vestiges of youthfulness seeming to be long gone.

On arriving, the palace seemed as it always did at this event. There were as usual torches lighting the steps but this year braziers had been placed on every fourth step, with the pages who helped the guests from their boats, standing close to them for warmth between their duties.

Without expectation, just merely assuming, Christos once inside the great hall thought he would be seated somewhere near the new duke, the duke's widow, and the dignitaries and emissaries from other states and countries.

Instead, he was placed half-way down the long table behind a giant floral display. On his left, he had the deaf wife of a now long-deceased head of the city council, and to his right the overweight daughter, with a face like a pumpkin, of the merchant who supplied the duke's foodstuffs. She even had the audacity to ask him who he was, and when he told her she was none the wiser.

Christos managed a rare smile to himself, for here he was one year after being part of the inner circle of the most influential people in the civilised world and now, just twelve months later he sat between two women with the charm, vivacity, and wit of dead fish.

Christos picked at the various dishes as they came his way, the rich, spicy, and bizarre foods arrived but he had little appetite. Unlike the two ladies either side of him, especially pumpkin face, who devoured every scrap on every plate as if she had never eaten before, though her ample proportions showed that not to be the case.

The entertainers were almost identical to the previous year except the musicians did not seem as good. Then after what seemed a very long time, the speeches began with introductions from the man in the golden hat, who Christos never saw from one year's party to the next.

Then finally the new duke got up to speak. Almost straight away, he complemented Veraccio who was seated nearby, on the truly magnificent panel he had created eulogizing in paint his father's life.

At this, of course, everyone stood and applauded the young duke's noble act, his perfect taste and discernment in choosing the artist he had, and Veraccio himself. He took the accolades in what was meant to be a rather coy manner, but Christos knew differently and shortly afterwards Christos took a boat home.

Winter with its darkness and cold seemed to go on for longer than ever. Felipe and Carlo assisted Christos on the pictures he had to do, but the energy he had was slipping away, and more and more his thoughts turned inwards.

Angelica saw what was happening, although she did not fully understand it, and tried her best to bring life and joy in this hard season to both Christos and the house itself. She arranged green foliage and winter fruits and berries on the table and lit candles and made sure the fires burned brightly. She made soups and dishes with spices and wine, but the torpor that was enveloping her master and friend she could not arrest. She observed his retreat into himself, and felt both helpless and sad.

Spring arrived and took the frost off the glass of the windows but not the cold out of Christos. He did what he had to do but rarely more and now seldom left the house, then only occasionally to attend a city meeting, but he missed more of those than he attended.

Work and commissions still arrived, not in the number or scale in which they had had, but there was still enough to do. It was Felipe who ran the studio in Moon Street, ordering materials, getting frames made, corresponding with clients and collecting payments, and doing with his brother most of the painting.

One beautiful late spring day the house had a surprise visitor, the physician Mondino. With his usual flurry, he bounded into the house, his energy as always seemed that of a far younger man.

He was not familiar with Felipe and his brother so on entering the studio he enquired in his seemingly blunt forthright manner who they were.

The two were taken aback at this old man's directness and sense of superiority.

They had no sooner given their names, which he seemed to take no regard of when he asked where Master Christos was.

Before they could answer, Angelica hearing a new voice appeared from the kitchen.

Mondino, with a flashing smile, asked her the same question, and in the same breath asked what the wondrous aroma from her kitchen was, and again without pausing for an answer sat himself down in readiness for lunch.

In her quiet way, Angelica explained that Christos was in his rooms and although he might not join them, there was crab and fish stew and that it would be ready in a few moments.

Felipe and Carlo joined Mondino at the table. Their morning had been long and difficult, repainting the head of a saint on a lime wood panel that had been sent to them with water damage caused when the roof of the chapel it had come from leaked, depositing a slimy liquid onto its surface.

Angelica laid out four large white flat oval dishes on the table, four ornate silver spoons, a basket containing a sliced rectangular loaf, four finely made crystal glasses, and one of the few remaining bottles of Master Paulo's wine. Then she returned from the kitchen, holding by its two handles, a white tureen with a knob on the lid in the shape of a pineapple, out of one side stuck the end of a serving spoon. This she placed in the centre of the table and on removing the lid, the aroma that Mondino had commented on filled the room. Angelica deftly served portions into the four dishes.

When Mondino asked if Christos would be with them soon, for he was eager to start eating, Felipe spoke, "No sir, Angelica will take his meal up to his rooms as she has done for the past few months."

That bought a noticeable silence from the physician.

When the tureen had been emptied, the wine drunk, mostly by the doctor, and the bread consumed, the physician gave his thanks to Angelica for such a tasty dish and without any thought of asking or needing permission, stood from the table and headed up the stairs to Christos's rooms to see for himself from what sort of malady the painter was suffering.

Pausing on the landing outside the wooden door that led to the suite of rooms that Christos occupied, Mondino cast his mind back to when he was here to treat his old friend Paulo after his fall. Christos, although a mere youth from the countryside, had been so helpful and attentive.

He knocked on the door but there was no reply from within, so his bony fingers slowly pushed the door open.

On entering, he found himself in almost complete darkness as the curtains and shutters were tightly closed, but when his eyes became used to the lack of light, he discerned the flickering yellow glow of a candle in the next room.

Moving quietly across the richly patterned rug, he saw Christos' head bowed, his hair long and dishevelled with his white shirt open by several buttons showing a body that looked old and scrawny.

Mondino spoke quietly, for he could see his young friend was in a bad way, "Christos, hello it's me Mondino." He rested his hand on his shoulder, "What has become of you, what is so wrong that I find you in this state?"

Christos as if waking from a dream, lifted his head and with a slow recognition, raised a slight smile.

Mondino pulled up a chair and sat down, taking the almost lifeless hand of Christos in his, feeling his pulse which was slow and faint.

"What has bought this state of affairs about? When I saw you at the funeral, you seemed your normal self and that was not that long ago. I see you have lost weight and are obviously not eating the delicious food your maid prepares. Why, my friend, on such a beautiful day as today are you sitting in the dark with the shutters closed? It's as if someone close has died."

Mondino was not expecting answers from any of these questions, he was simply thinking aloud trying to form some reason for the melancholia that seemed to have enveloped the man in front of him.

"Everything seems futile and pointless, more than that I cannot say," Christos said, looking down at the floor.

The physician noticed a small tear fall from the now lustreless eyes of the artist. Mondino stiffened his lip while observing his friend, and now patient.

Patting his hand in a pretence of normality and jollity, he said, "We will soon have you full of vigour and energy again, leave it to me. Tomorrow I will call again if that is alright with you."

Christos nodded meekly.

"We will start you back on the path to your former self."

Downstairs, Mondino asked some questions of Felipe and Angelica to get a fuller picture of what might have caused his patient's condition but their answers seemed vague. Not that they were being unhelpful or disinterested in their master's state, but just that they did not really know.

Mondino gleaned it had come about slowly, rather like a fog that rolls in from the sea and blankets the shore.

"Alright I will call again in the morning," he said. "I would have commenced treatment now but I do not have my instruments with me, and I also need to prepare a tonic for him overnight."

He walked briskly home. He had lived in this city all his life and was nearly seventy, or so he thought. He was a known figure amongst those he passed and since a young man, although he had no false arrogance, he'd been treated with respect and deference and had never been attacked by rogues or villains. Though he often carried gemstones more valuable than gold, his presence and knowing eyes deterred any such troubles.

After a quarter of one hour, he reached the weathered oak door of his house on d'Oro Street, and separating a large iron key from the cluster on the ring he took from his pocket, opened the door with a sense of harmony. For he had, while walking, counted in the back of his mind the number of steps it had taken, which was one thousand five hundred and ninety-seven.

Perfect, he thought to himself and smiling he entered the hallway and was greeted by his two cats that rubbed against his ankles.

Mondino knew the course his treatment of Christos would take. He needed to balance his patient's humours so he would let some blood, in conjunction with that he would revive his spirits with an elixir.

He entered his untidy laboratory lined with shelves that had upon them bottles, jars and vats of various colours containing all the ingredients he would need.

First in a blackcurrant alcohol solution, he added a distillation of Agarwood which had a beautiful complex and pleasing scent to aid the reacquaintance of his patient Christos with himself, and in the process relieve stress.

Then a quantity of nutmeg which would help cure and stop disease. It was even mooted that it could ward off the plague. Mondino was not so sure but it would clear any fungus within his system and in all likelihood increase his ardour.

Next he added a rare ingredient, hog plum. This he boiled and pulped and added an amount that would aid in cleansing the body of impurities and restore balance.

After that he added the ground leaves of bamboo to work as a stimulant and general tonic, he thought of including its boiled sap but on reflection decided it unnecessary, so added some ground bamboo root instead, which would aid rest and ease anxiety. What a wonderful and useful plant the bamboo was, he mused.

His elixir was now almost complete, a few drops of costus to kill off infection, the seeds from the White Sal tree, some valerian ground from its root, and finally a spoonful of Saint John's wort to alter Christos' melancholic humour.

The mixture complete, he transferred it into five dark blue octagonal sided glass bottles. Into each of which he pushed a cork and then shook vigorously. Finally, on five small labels, he wrote Christos' name, the date, and the words, 'Take a spoonful twice a day'. With that complete, he went to bed.

The morning so far had been very satisfactory, he had drunk fruit juice and eaten some stewed apricots for breakfast. He had fed his cats some fish, who after they had eaten, promptly ignored him, stretched themselves and left to explore the neighbourhood via a hole he had cut in the back door.

Having prepared what he thought would get Christos out of his lethargic state the day before, he read for a while and at nine-thirty picked up his bag, locked his front door and walked to Moon Street.

Felipe and his brother nodded and mumbled good mornings when the physician arrived, continuing their work.

To Angelica who had cleared breakfast away and was potting some fruit into glass jars, Mondino enquired, "Did he eat anything this morning?"

"Next to nothing, sir," Angelica replied.

With that, the physician made his way up the stairs to Christos' rooms picking up a broom as he went.

Today the curtains had been partially drawn and Christos was putting on a clean shirt as Mondino entered.

"Good morning, dear doctor. What a pleasant morning."

The change from the previous afternoon, Mondino noted, was almost total. "Yes it is a fine morning to be alive but my visit yesterday suggested to me that I think you need a bit of a tonic after the long winter, so I have prepared an elixir that will do you immense good, but I would also suggest Master Christos that first, we breathe your veins."

Then before he had time to protest, Mondino had put his hands on Christos' shoulders, sat him down in a chair and rolled up his sleeve.

Despite Christos' fame and celebrity the older man still held sway and respect over the artist.

"Now I am sure you have seen this done before, but if you haven't then what I want you to do is hold the broomstick as tightly as possible to raise the veins in your arm. If you do not like the sight of blood look away and concentrate on gripping the rod. I am going to tie this short leather strap just above your elbow," which he had taken from his worn bag, "to aid in our endeavour."

Christos went to speak but the physician cut him short sensing resistance, "Relax, my dear friend, it will not take long, we are merely going to take a small amount to balance your humours. Remember I have probably performed this procedure more times than all the other physicians in this city put together."

With the strap firmly tied, Mondino returned to his bag and produced a thin long-bladed knife and a small copper bowl with a handle. Pulling up a chair he sat down opposite his patient and gently but firmly holding his arm, he made a small incision from which the blood slowly ran around the arm into the cup that Mondino held underneath.

Christos was not keen on the sight of blood, especially his own, and sat back in his chair quiet and slightly ashen-faced.

The physician put a gauze on the small wound on his arm and told Christos to hold it in place, then he poured some spirit on the blade of the knife replaced it in his bag and took out one of the blue bottles.

"Now I want you to take this every day till I tell you to stop." He poured an amount onto a spoon which he had produced from his pocket, having picked it up as he passed through the kitchen. The thought had crossed his mind several times throughout his life that he had the stealth to be a thief.

Dutifully Christos opened his mouth as Mondino poured the spoonful of the purple blackcurrant tonic into it.

"See, it is not disagreeable is it? For your own sake, my dear friend, take it twice a day, first and last thing. I shall leave the other bottles in the safekeeping of your wonderful maid and cook who is a real treasure to this house, for I have to travel south to visit an old friend an alchemist from Arabia, who has sent word he needs to see me."

With that, he turned, waved his hand in the air in a gesture of farewell and on negotiating the stairs, returned to the kitchen and instructed Angelica to keep the remaining four bottles in a safe place and to keep a check on whether her master was following his instructions.

"Finally, before I go, I wish to banish any evil spirits that may have entered here." He rummaged in his bag and retrieved a bunch of twigs and leaves tied together with blue twine. "We together, are going to set fire to these herbs."

Taking Angelica by the hand, he led her to the main door that opened out onto the waterway. Giving her the bunch of herbs, he took a flint from his pocket and lit a spark under the dry plant which rather than combust, smouldered.

"Right my girl, start gently waving it."

Which rather excitedly Angelica did, for this eminent man was taking notice of her, which most did not.

The smoke wafted into the ground floor hallway and curled its aromatic perfume up the stairs, and out of the doorway in sinuous silvery grey swirls where it hovered above the still waters before vanishing.

When the bunch of twigs had almost burnt away Mondino smiled at Angelica as a father would with a daughter, for her attention was totally caught up in the activity. "It is burning close to your hand," he said. "Throw what remains into the water."

His words breaking her trance, she looked up at his genial expression and did as he asked, hearing the faint hiss as the water quenched the burning herbs.

"I will return in a month, please look after him."

Angelica smiled slightly.

~ Chapter Fourteen ~

The physician's visit seemed to improve Christos' mood and something of the way it used to be returned to Moon Street. Angelica noted that Christos was taking his tonic, and he had also returned to eating his meals with the rest of them. There was a general air of happiness in the house that had not been there for a long time.

That was until the evening of the fifth day of the month, when Christos returned from a city council meeting earlier than expected, entered the house in a rage and went straight to his rooms, slamming the door behind him.

A while later, Angelica timidly holding a tray of food, knocked gently on Christos' door, for she did not really want to knock at all, but there was no reply.

Wondering quite what to do, she knocked again but slightly louder, still there was no response; then concerned if he was alright, she turned the handle and the door opened.

He was standing with his back to her, hands clenched into fists on the table in front of him and with his head bent down, muttering to himself.

She took a pace into the room but hearing her step, he turned and shouted at her to get out, then picking up the nearest thing to him, which was Mondino's elixir, he threw it at her. The glass bottle hit the wall and shattered, its purple fluid running down the wall in rivulets.

Shocked, Angelica dropped the tray, started crying and fled back down the stairs. She found her shawl and ran out of the front door, vowing never to return.

Felipe and his brother had heard the shouting, unable to calm or stop the maid as she rushed through the studio, they looked at each other questioningly.

The following morning Angelica did not arrive and there was no breakfast laid out. So the brothers fried some eggs, cut some slices off the half-eaten round loaf from yesterday with the crisscross pattern on it, fried it in the oil from the eggs and started work.

Later that day Carlo went around to Angelica's to find out why she had left in the way she had.

Breaking into tears again, she explained what had happened but added almost as an afterthought how much she cared for Christos and only wanted to help him.

Carlo, who was short and a little plump, asked Angelica if she would come back as he and his brother missed her being around. Not least for the tasty food she made, though he did not say that.

Angelica said she would think about it, which gave Carlo hope that the pies, stews, soups, and other delicious foods she made would soon come their way again.

Four days had passed with no return of Angelica and no appearance by Christos, but the brothers had noticed that Christos had been coming down to the kitchen in the dead of night to eat a little food.

While in a tavern one evening, Felipe met a clerk he knew that worked in the city hall who happened to be taking notes on the council meeting the day Christos had returned home in such a foul mood.

The clerk explained, "The meeting was about the selection of an artist to paint a vast canvas depicting the history of the city. As was well known within the corridors and anterooms of city hall, Christos expected the commission to go to him. As the most famous and renowned artist of the city and on the council as overseer of all artistic endeavour within its precincts, it was not an unreasonable thought."

Felipe nodded, eager to hear the rest.

The clerk continued, "But all decisions great or small taken by the council have to be voted upon. Of the twenty-seven councillors present, the vast majority seemed in favour of Christos undertaking the work."

Felipe began to guess what had happened.

The clerk went on, "Before the vote was taken, the young Duke of Castello arrived, he appeared to have had too much wine and with his arrival, the mood amongst the councillors changed. He suggested in a subtly sarcastic way, that such a magnificent and illustrious artist as Christos, surely had too much to do and with so many of his works around the city already, perhaps another artist might bring a variety and freshness to the project – such as Veraccio. Just his humble opinion of course." The clerk laughed.

"The vote taken shortly after this short intervention resulted in all the council voting for Veraccio to commence as early as possible. Christos at that point lost control, banged his fist down onto the table and left without a word." The clerk added, "I did see a wry smile on the young duke's face as Christos left."

"I now understand," said Felipe. "When is Master Veraccio due to commence this new work?"

"In the new year," replied the clerk, and Felipe bought him another drink thinking over the news.

The summer passed, the winds freshened, and the days shortened. Felipe and his brother did not rush through the work they had to do. They saw that Christos had lost his energy and vitality and new commissions were getting fewer and fewer, so they made arrangements to leave Moon Street towards the end of the year to work for Veraccio, but this they kept to themselves.

Angelica returned, in part because of more persuasion from Carlo with his desire for her cooking, but mostly because she worried about the health and welfare of Christos, who Carlo told her rarely left his rooms and said virtually nothing when they met.

Mondino on his return from the alchemist visited the studio to see how his patient was responding, but Christos turned on him, calling him a charlatan and a quack, so the physician looked him in the eye and told him he was a blind and stupid man with less understanding than a goat.

On leaving, Mondino stopped by the kitchen door giving Angelica a hug and a kiss on the cheek, at which she blushed, and told her quietly that if she ever needed him to just send word.

Two weeks into December, there were snow flurries in the air and Christos, on one of those very rare days, was in the studio painting the eyes of a noblewoman from a city to the west.

It was towards the end of that day when Felipe broke the news of their departure, explaining that Christos had been a good master to work for but there was less and less to do. As he and his brother had considerably less wealth than he, they must look to their futures and so they had taken up good positions with Antonio Veraccio, which at the least guaranteed them work for the best part of the following year.

Christos stopped painting and sat down or rather slumped down in his chair.

The sight of the man who had once been the most renowned artist in Europe, sitting silently, still and barely breathing, with head and eyes cast down at the paint-stained floorboards brought a feeling of sadness to Felipe. A sense of the fickle hand of fortune and fate which could befall anyone crossed his mind. All he could say was, "Sorry, but we have made our decision."

Three weeks later the brothers left with their few belongings, they had called up to Christos to say goodbye but there had been no reply.

Angelica was there, and despite the cold, stood with the brothers in the small courtyard for a little while as they promised to call around soon. As a parting gift, she gave them each a rabbit pie she had made the previous evening wrapped in blue check cloth, and at the gate, Carlo turned and smiled warmly to her before closing it behind him.

Over the next few weeks Christos kept very still, he slept a lot and usually woke in the early hours and when awake, sat in the same chair with the events of his life flickering back and forth in his mind. He kept still as if it was protection, a preventative from a cascade of something unknown enveloping him.

When he did go down to the kitchen or into the bathroom, it needed some prior thought for a state of readiness to be brought about via a set of weird illogical equations.

The thought of not painting again was constantly with him and with no commissions coming in, this was a possibility, and if there was nothing to paint then no money would arrive.

So one morning, having thought of it for hours, Christos went to all his secret hiding places, under floorboards, boxes on top of wardrobes, inside hollowed-out books, behind six loose bricks in a wall of the attic and many more, and collected together all his coins and valuables that he had hidden away and spread them out on his table.

He placed the large gold coins and then the small gold coins in piles on top of each other, and there were many piles. Next the silver coinage, large, small, thick and thin, again placed one on top of another in multiples of ten, then the copper coins and other lesser metals and the French coins from his time with the king and his cousin, they were beautify stamped and he had several hundred of them. Then finally personal gifts he had received, like a brooch set with pearls, a dark green bag containing sparkling diamonds, and then emeralds, rubies, sapphires both ice and sea blue, and several handfuls of other semi-precious gems which were all the colours one could imagine.

At the reassuring sight of his wealth spread out before him, he deliberately widened his fingers letting a few of the gems fall to the table below, knocking over some of the piles of coins. A half-smile creased the skin on his tightly drawn face and he felt full, as if after a large meal, and he sat for a time enjoying the fullness his amassed fortune gave him.

With Angelica away for the day, Christos stirred himself and started replacing his hoard into its dark and secretive places in the fabric of the house.

He found a new place as well, for he thought the more places his hoard was hidden, the safer it would be. So in the corner of the reception hall, he lifted a flagstone that had always been not quite level. He pushed a sturdy knife from the kitchen into the join with the next flag and holding it vertically with one hand, scraped an indentation in the hard, compacted, red earth beneath. Then he took the green pouch of diamonds from his coat and nestled them into the new hollow. Then he let the heavy stone fall back into place, and when he stood on it, the unevenness was gone.

Christos thought about his age, though he was not entirely sure what it was, and his physical condition, and calculated the number of years he was likely to live, although that was very imprecise as anything could happen at any time. Then with simple division, he worked out how much money he had for each remaining year, even if he grew very old. He saw it would be ample, with no hint of poverty.

Later that evening the contentment he had felt when counting his money had gone.

Christos contemplated the house, it had bars on the lower windows, the large door to the waterway had bolts at the top and bottom and had a lock that took a key that was larger than his hand. The rear door, leading into the small courtyard, had a single bolt and a lock and key, but much smaller than the other.

These thoughts occurred because now he was alone in the house, with the days of Paulo and the others long gone. The theft by Arcolano and Jacamo still stung, for they had never been apprehended and so no punishment dealt to them. What if in the dead of night, they returned, he thought, and maybe with others to help, could he defend himself? He was no swordsman, and insecurity started swirling in his mind. He sat in his chair unable to get into bed.

Angelica arrived the following morning having been to the market. She busied herself in the kitchen preparing soup, and while that was simmering, cleared out the grates and lit fires, for the house was stone cold. She knew going up to Christos' rooms with food would be met by rejection, and she was also slightly frightened in case he lost his temper again, so she merely made enough noise to let him know she was downstairs.

Later that day when she had done all she could, with the house warmer and food cooked in the kitchen, she called up a goodbye. With the usual sense of disappointment, she received no reply and let herself out by the back door.

This was the way it was for many months, with her doing what she could to aid her friend in his isolation, and he, when she had left, taking a little of the food she had prepared and leaving some coins in the kitchen to buy whatever was needed.

Occasionally when Christos went down to get food from the kitchen, he would stand in his studio looking at the empty wall that had held so many wonderful pictures. It felt as if it had all been in another life, a dream, pictures painted not by him but by some other him, someone he no longer knew. An immense sadness filled his being, for that time that was now gone.

Winter had seemed long and Christos nearly always felt a chill in his bones despite the layers of clothes he had taken to wearing. Unknowingly, winter and its dull light and darkness had become his ally, for when spring arrived, he shunned the brightness and warmth of its days, and with the shutters and curtains drawn, tried to sleep through them and only awaken at nightfall.

There were odd times when he would open the shutters slightly and look out for a while and although what he saw seemed familiar, he felt no connection to it and just watched blankly.

On one occasion after taking some food from the kitchen, he ventured into the courtyard and for the first time in many months, felt the breeze against his skin. But it brought no joy nor any sadness, it was just there, as he was. He watched the fresh green leaves flutter on the tree but nothing stirred in him, and he turned, locked the door behind him, climbed the stairs, and went back to his rooms.

Christos was forgotten, his neighbours in Moon Street had stopped gossiping about him some while ago as there was nothing new to rekindle their interest. They, of course, observed the maid coming and going but she by her demeanour gave nothing away, walking as she did with her eyes cast down in her contained way. They knew he was alive because she came and went, and no body had been brought out. They also assumed he was not ill, as no doctors were called, so although peculiar, the shuttered house and its occupant became what was normal. It had been replaced with more interesting speculations.

Much the same feeling had been adopted by those on the city council whose meetings he now never attended. He had always had an arrogance about him, a superior air, that in some ways had been justified. He had lacked humility and made them feel like they moved in smaller realms than he, so it was no loss, it simply was better without him around and no messenger was sent to make enquiries as to his wellbeing.

The artists and suppliers he had known and used held similar views, concocting their own stories of his retreat from the world, some saying he had lost his mind, others that he practised dark arts and needed solitude; and one tale that persisted for a while, was that he had fallen while carrying boiling water, scalded himself and was now grotesquely disfigured and that the light caused him pain.

He became forgotten.

Christos had become unaware of the passing of time but sometimes in the hours and days alone, his mind, without his wish, recalled the bright sunny days of his youth which now seemed so far away and it deepened the empty feeling he seemed always to have. A feeling so crushing in its power over him that he believed it came not from within himself but from some external force, a force so overwhelming and dark that death itself seemed a brighter prospect, a better place to be, and this thought of death gained in appeal as time passed.

He would wake and find that tears were running down his cheeks and the darkness would still be there, ever-present, a dark fog from which he could find no end – perhaps that had no end.

Angelica saw he picked at the food which she left for him, the amounts eaten were what a child would eat, and she worried about the man whom she had known for so long, since he had first arrived from the countryside as almost a boy. She felt powerless to give him the affection and love she knew he needed.

The days ticked by in their procession, there was blue skies, rain, grey cloud, breezes, storms, thunder, lightning, sun, and moonshine with twinkling stars; but in the solitary world that Christos was in, there was only darkness. He thought of escape from the crushing sensation he constantly lived with but mostly he was paralysed by it, inert and trapped as he searched the possibilities of his escape from the hold of this monster.

He could go into the attic, open a window, climb out and let himself fall and crash to the ground but he might live, mangled and broken, almost unable to move or feed himself, and then the monster would return and he would be a captive within himself with all escape rendered impossible and taken from his hands. A dagger in the heart was another method, another choice, there were numerous sharp knives within the building but would his frail form find the courage and strength to perform such an act, could he summon the will to feel the pain of the cold steel slicing through his body to end his torments. He doubted it and felt worse as a result. Drowning, in such a place as this city with its myriad waterways, seemed at first thought, an excellent way of pulling a veil over his life but it felt wrong and would be very public when his body was found. This business, this cessation he did not want to share, to be hauled onto some quayside like a rotting fish, was not the way.

The choice, by process of elimination, to end this world had to be poison. Christos thought he would be able to die in his bed without any physical signs of injury and it would be private and not require any nerve or courage, but which poison, arsenic? He could get this from his paint merchant included in an order so as not to arouse suspicion, and if any questions were asked, he could say that he was experimenting in making a new green. He could ask Angelica to get some belladonna berries from the apothecaries, again there would be no suspicion as women used it to make their eyes more alluring and beautiful.

With both these possibilities now in his mind, Christos felt he had gained an advantage, won a victory and found some clear light over the malevolent force that had been plaguing him for so long. Although still unhappy and alone, he felt somewhat better and that night, he finally slept.

~ Chapter Fifteen ~

When he awoke his enemy was already there waiting. Christos felt immediately that the fight was over, with futility, loss and emptiness filling his being, he lay flat on his back on his bed as if knocked to the ground. He cried out like a lost child, pleading for help.

"You have forgotten me," A voice said, sounding in his head. "You thought me of little worth, you discarded me for fine and rich fabric and abandoned what I gave you, thinking I was of little consequence, a mere artefact of no importance. You consigned me to a dark and long-forgotten place and sorely undervalued my importance in your life. Nevertheless, I am not bitter and hold no grudge against you. I wonder if in the piteous state you find yourself in, you even know who or what is speaking to you. I am that 'deserved gift' that was given to you. A day that feels so long ago to you now.

"I am the cloak that the old lady Antonina passed to you. I whose words ring in your mind, brought you dreams of happiness and joy in past days. I was your companion, spread across your bed, shaping your thoughts and energy, till you became the person you were, but then you and I went our separate ways. It happened a little at a time, but you were set on the course you took and have now arrived at your destination, but I think it is not where you expected to be.

"You became what you wanted, your talent and skills were acknowledged, and with that success, came fame and fortune, but you became greedy and avaricious. Gluttony was with you every day and changed your form, you became wrathful, venting your anger on those around you so that they turned away and no longer wished to know you. Then you allowed lust to take over your senses, assuming in your arrogance you could possess whoever you wished, regardless of how they felt towards you, and latterly you have made friends with sloth and laziness, enjoying their indolent company.

"But pride was the first of this list of faults you allowed into your life, and success, that fickle mistress, led you to believe you were better than all other men, and you strutted through this place with vanity. Though this is but a cracked mirror of your reality, which men of humility and wisdom see as a delusion, and smiled at its and your conceit, but like a fish, you had swallowed the hook and were caught.

"The paradox for you, my dear friend, was that the greater and better you did in the world of flesh and blood, the poorer became your spirit or soul or whatever you call it, but it is that part of every man that never leaves him and that in an ever-changing world will always be constant.

"You have been silent for some little time now while you have been hearing my voice, and I wonder if what you have heard was a surprise, if it was, my old friend, then we will have to work even harder to restore you to your former self. Have no doubts however, we will achieve that and much more.

"This dark time you have endured from now onwards will not get worse. Yes, there will be days when you feel yourself slipping back into its clutches, but we will make steady progress, as the sun does across the morning sky, until all darkness is gone and light will be the realm in which you live. Do not say anything for there is no need, I am going now for a short while but do not fear I am nearby, and I will return after you have had time to think of what I have said."

Christos had been stunned by the words that had gone through his mind, supposedly said by the cloak he once had, it had been so long since he had thought of it and even longer since he had seen it, and he was not even sure if he still had it or where it might be.

After a time and with deliberation, Christos placed one foot and then the other on the floor, aware of his measured breathing, he felt the weight of his legs upon it, and he slowly stood.

After a pause, he turned towards the window and half drew back the curtains so that lines and beads of sunlight entered the room through the slats of the shutters, the light illuminating the dust that filled the room.

Then at the same slow pace, Christos went to the first cupboard and looked inside it, pulling open drawers, looking under clothes he had not seen or worn for a long time, opening boxes of all sizes and colours which had faded with age, and pushing to one side the garments hanging from rails. This search continued all morning without success.

He looked in every possible place within his rooms but did not find what he wanted. The search had taken some time and the exertion, which he was not used to, had created a sensation he had not felt for a long while, namely hunger.

He descended the stairs to the kitchen, not in his usual quiet and slightly furtive way but with unexpected energy and vigour that felt very good.

Angelica was just about to leave as Christos came through the door and both were surprised to encounter each other. Angelica, for her part, was surprised to see Christos at all, and his manner seemed so changed from the previous months, he seemed more like his old self beyond the mask of care he still wore. He was surprised too, that he was face to face with the person who without any questions had provided for him for so long, and he felt almost shy as he greeted her.

Angelica smiled while holding back the emotion she felt, and taking off her jacket, she sliced some bread and took a selection of cold meats and some cheese from the larder and placed it on the table. As she turned away to get something for him to drink Christos said, "Will you sit with me, Angelica? I really would like your company."

They did not speak a great deal during the simple meal but Angelica was pleased to see his appetite had somewhat returned, and when he had finished, he touched her hand and gave her a warm smile in thanks and said, "I am trying to find something so I must take my leave." She felt a happiness that she had not experienced for some time.

Back in his rooms, the blackness, the monster, made a return and tried to take hold of his thoughts and body, but the words spoken to him by the cloak earlier in the day came through and held sway.

Christos feeling free of gloom had an inkling of an idea and made his way to the top of the house, to the attic room he had once shared with Stuardo.

The door squeaked as he opened it and he found it filled with light which made him narrow his eyes, for there were no curtains to close. No one had used the room for some time, and the two beds were stripped bare, with their sheets and covers folded into rectangular piles at the foot of each.

Christos sat down on the bed that had been his. Memories flooded back and the thoughts of his youth and his first days in this house seemed like yesterday. However, he knew it was a long time ago and he felt a sadness about the passing of his life.

He broke away from those feelings and with his newly found energy, stood and opened the cupboard where he and Stuardo had kept their clothes. It was empty except for what he had been looking for, there crumpled on the floor in the corner, was the cloak, his cloak.

He smiled a wry smile as he bent and picked it up. It felt the same, its weight, its feel, the colour which had not changed, with the blue still as deep and strong. He held it out in front of him and let its length drop towards the floor and there were no creases in it. He gathered it towards himself and pressed his face against it, as a girl might do with a doll. Holding it there, he felt a sense of relief as if returning home from a long and arduous journey, the cloak bringing back memories of Antonina and the smell of the bread she had sold on her stall.

Settling back on the bed once again, he put the cloak over himself and letting its weight fall upon him, closed his eyes and fell asleep.

When he woke, he knew that it had not been sleep to hide from fears and run from anxiety but a sleep of true rest and refreshment and of dreams that sparkle and shine with joy and happiness. This he had missed for so long.

A sense of energy and good feeling ran through him, and lying there, on that simple bed in that plain unadorned room with its bare floorboards and faded walls, he felt lighter and younger.

Then the voice of the cloak spoke to him again. "I said I would be back. I never break a promise and I always keep my word, and you have found me again. I was never far away and I had patience because I have been around for a long time. The scurrying of man is nothing new to me, with their vain pursuits of glory and wealth.

"So my friend, the black monster you thought held you so tight has started to disappear like the early morning mist and allowed the sun to shine through. Is it not a wonderful feeling? You see your plea was answered. They always are. Maybe not directly, as one wishes, but the answer is never worse, just maybe different.

"Heartfelt pleas only require the person to truly want what it is they are asking for. Gold, diamonds, wealth, things of the visible world will not be granted, because they, by their very nature, do not endure, no matter how great the palace or kingdom or trove of wealth, these things will vanish. It is the invisible things that will come to you, happiness when you are sad, friendship when you are lonely, warmth in your heart when it feels like stone, and light and joy when all is blackness and despair.

"So now that you have found me again, I am going to tell you something about myself. I am not made from any ordinary cloth, I do not wear out, I do not fade or fray, and yet I am as old as man himself.

"Also let me tell you this, you followed your dream to be an artist, someone who creates images of real things in two dimensions with skill and artistry. You, Christos, who convinced the world that your depictions were valid and real and that the messages you conveyed through paint on canvas, wood, or plaster should be taken into our beings, affect our thoughts, and direct us in ways that words cannot do. You who have this understanding of symbols and the symbolic never took more than a passing glance at the patterns that wise men through the ages had attached to me.

"But you were young when I came into your life and with your dizzying success, I was put to one side and you did not see me. Now that you are older and somewhat wiser, look and what do you see? Circles, dashes, dots, lines put together to form different shapes and patterns, but they are not as arbitrary or random as you may think. These symbols in their varying colours are distillations of universal wisdom, they are no less than the wisdom of the world, and when you understand them you will know what makes a man great or small, wise or not, special or just ordinary.

"There are many symbols woven into me and I will explain some. First let us start with this violet circle with its spokes bent at angles around the outer edge of the wheel and the five-pointed star within, with a yellow stone at the centre. It is the symbol of transformation and rebirth, it tells of the universe revolving around the star, which is you, and represents you moving from one state to another in that universe and within your being, which is constantly changing. Then there is light, the sun, represented by the pure yellow of this stone which brings the ability to sublimate matter that alchemists have long sought to do, that is the transmutation of base metals into gold, but you can perform that act not with metals but with your very self, and when you truly understand, you will be able to transform others, and that is a wonderful gift.

"Lastly look at these two interlocking key shapes in yellow, it's the symbol for wisdom, ingenuity, intelligence, and patience. Both parts of this sign could be taken apart or put together so they overlap and appear unified as one, but the symbol's simplicity is concealing its complexity, as with the wise and intelligent man, he can see a problem and find a solution, but because he has wisdom he can express the answer so even a child would gain understanding, another true gift.

"I am not going to speak to you again for a while," the cloak said, "but look after me this time, it was not good in that dark place."

With a lightness of heart and step, Christos moved to the window and held it open, letting the southern breeze coming off the sea enter and fill the attic. He put the cloak over his shoulder and went down to his rooms, he did not know what he was going to do with the rest of his day but as a start to whatever it might be, he drew back the curtains, opened the windows as he had in the attic, and fastened the shutters to the walls outside.

It did not occur to him, but it was a sign to those outside that the recluse, the madman, the alchemist, whatever they might have been calling him was back in their midst, and it felt good as he stood there watching life along the waterway unfurl beneath him.

As he looked out of the window, a man of what he assumed was his age, dressed in green with an orange scarf tied around his head and with a basket on his shoulder in which something was moving, looked up as he heard the shutters being fastened in place. He nodded in an open and friendly way and Christos slightly taken aback, raised his hand showing his palm in response, and with the gesture, the weight of the blackness that had been his companion for so long receded further, as a bad dream does on waking.

Looking around, Christos started clearing the debris left from his black time, replacing books on shelves, picking up clothing, removing the bedding and placing it in a heap outside his door, till all the miasmic emanations, with the help of warm currents from the desserts far away, had gone.

The bedding he replaced with crisp clean sheets and a new cover from a cupboard in his bathroom. That done, he took the cloak off his shoulder and with care folded it in half and laid it with almost reverence across the bottom of his bed. Then he turned, picked up his old bedding and went down to the kitchen and placed it all in a chest behind the door.

The exertions had renewed his appetite, and he sat with an apple, some cheese and a beaker of grape juice, and savoured what he thought were his achievements of the day.

Then he wandered into the empty studio and thought of Angelica who had left several hours ago and he wanted to see her but knew he would have to wait till the morning.

With the day in its final part, Christos went to the ground floor, opened the main door and stood in its opening. Two women walked by in conversation and as they passed, they glanced his way. He smiled and when they had gone, he looked up into the cerulean sky and watched a group of swallows soaring and diving with their effortless ease. He stayed in the doorway till the light had gone, and that night his sleep was deep and restful.

Christos woke before dawn. The shutters he had left open, and early morning sounds of this city by the sea started entering his room. Seagulls squawking, the gentle sound of the wind, the sea breaking against the quayside some way off, and now as he lay still, attentively listening, the voices raised in greeting of those up early going to the fish market to buy and sell, and the sound of the bells of the little church around the corner.

Refreshed and with a sense of excitement running through his veins, he dressed quickly, pulling on some red britches and a white shirt which he tucked in but mostly left undone as if to do all the buttons would be a waste of his seemingly precious time. In the bathroom he rubbed his teeth with his preferred mixture of ground eggshells, sage, and cream of tartar, then splashed his face with water, damping his long hair at the same time, then running his fingers through it and pushing it back across his head. Feeling clean, he went downstairs.

By now the first rays of light lit the studio walls. He thought about getting the house painted and cleaned as he went into the kitchen. There was very little there to eat and it would be three or four hours before Angelica arrived, so he went back into his rooms, took some coins off the table and went out the front door, locking it with the large key which he slipped into his pocket.

Christos set off along the waterfront to a bar that the fishermen used that served pancakes and coffee, and all this he did as though he did it every day, although he had not left Moon Street in many months.

The atmosphere was friendly and he struck up a conversation with an Arabic sailor over the quality of the food in this modest yet excellent place. Christos asked how long he had been in the city and where he had come from. The man had a sharp nose and green eyes and told of how he travelled here twice a year with spices, mostly saffron from the east.

He continued, moving his face closer to Christos' and lowering his voice to a whisper, "Although that is lucrative, the real cargo I sometimes bring with me is priceless, and for that, I get no monetary reward."

Christos looked at him puzzled and the Arab with a twinkle in his eye smiled. "Let me explain," he said, "For I know you will understand. I have been charged, or if you prefer, I have been blessed, for you see I and others before me are messengers, bringers of a sort of magic that even if they don't know it, men desire. I am able to change lives, solve the conundrums that plague man and alter their worlds, I bring understanding and wisdom."

Reaching inside his robe, he brought out an item wrapped in silk. Placing it on the table between them, he carefully laid the silk aside, revealing a small black rectangular stone a quarter the size of a playing card inscribed with a circle of lapis lazuli.

"This is just a minor treasure," the Arab said and placed it in Christos' hand.

"What is it?" Christos asked.

"This object will bring harmony to someone whose life is discordant."

"Who are you going to give it to?" asked Christos, as the Arab carefully rewrapped the black stone and replaced it in his robe.

"I will know that when I meet them, and if I don't and have to set sail before I find them, then I will place it for safekeeping until my next voyage but eventually the right person will appear to me."

"Why did you sit down with me to tell this story and show me this object?" Christos wondered.

"Because I knew you were a person with special qualities and would understand my mission, and also you are ready to know these things," the Arab replied with a knowing smile. "That is why."

"But if there is no monetary gain for you in finding a person to give that stone to, why do you do it?"

Laughing gently, the Arab placed his hand on the back of Christos' hand which was resting on the table. "Because, my friend, it is good to give, to pass on knowledge when someone is seeking it, to help create a better life for that person, who in turn, I hope, will do the same. That way this world we all share will be a better place. Although you may not understand this, I receive merit by giving, which makes my life have greater value and it also increases the energy which is in my being and hopefully emanates from me, so the selling of my cargo feeds my body and that of my family and friends and provides somewhere with comforts to live, but the giving of the things that bring knowledge, understanding, and wisdom, feeds my soul."

"I do understand," Christos said after a pause, "I, many years ago, was given a special gift that now I look back, changed my life, and although I ignored the value and worth of that gift for a long time, it has come and rescued me in just the last few days from a place to which no man should ever have to go to."

"What was that gift?" the Arab asked.

"A cloak of midnight blue decorated with patterns, shapes, and symbols of every colour, it guided me in the direction my life should follow and has now begun again."

"You were indeed given something of great value," said the Arab. "Such a gift will have made you a special person, which is why I was drawn to sit with you this while. Stay attuned to what it tells you and your life will be good, but for now I must say goodbye. I'm sure we will meet again."

Christos felt youthful as he left the small bar and walked back towards Moon Street. Unlocking the front door, which he let swing wide, he left it open as he went up the stairs into the studio. He stood looking at the main wall carrying the marks, ticks, and dashes of paint that never made it onto the finished paintings which were now somewhere else, perhaps hanging on walls in churches, palaces, grand houses or civic buildings.

Each residue of paint, each mark, told him instantly which picture it was from, when that particular mark was made, who made it, and even the weather and time of year. They, this collection of extra unwanted deposits of paint left upon the wall, told of his history since he had arrived from the country all those years ago. Although over time the wall had been whitewashed, they still were there in their varying degrees of clarity, and as he looked around the room, he noticed all the other traces of time. There on the easel, on the floor, the score on the table where Jacamo one day in temper had stuck his knife before being reprimanded by Paulo.

What a good man Paolo had been, like the father he had never known. As a tinge of melancholy was beginning to enter his mind, he heard footsteps on the flags below. Going to the top of the stairs, he saw Angelica entering with a basket over her arm and her flaxen hair moving gently on her shoulders. The nostalgic mood left him and he called out a greeting, at which she looked up and smiled.

Quickly he descended the stairs and taking the basket from her, took her arm, and although she needed no assistance, he helped her to the first floor. The attention did not go unnoticed by Angelica.

In the kitchen, they unpacked the food and Christos told her of his morning. His enthusiasm for his new state of wellbeing bubbled out of him with his plans to paint the house and recommence painting.

"Have you a commission?" Angelica asked.

"No, I have no commissions. I am going to paint what is important to me from now on and if the world out there likes it, then well and good, and if it doesn't, I really don't care."

"What have you in mind?"

"Well with your permission, I would like to paint you."

At that, Angelica dropped the lemons she was putting in a bowl. Turning to face Christos, she said, "That is the most wonderful thing anyone has ever said to me," and burst into tears.

Christos seeing her emotions overwhelming her, stepped forward and put his arm around her. Holding her close, he said, "It will be a beautiful picture."

~ Chapter Sixteen ~

Over the following weeks, the house was painted, floors were smoothed and varnished and the chimneys were swept. Angelica saw to it that the curtains were all taken down and washed, the kitchen and larder restocked, the furniture waxed and everywhere tidied and cleaned.

The malaise that had lain over the house and Christos himself was being vanquished, the dark closed atmosphere was replaced with the scent of flowers and the freshness of the sea air. In the studio Christos attended to his paints and brushes, the old and the dry paint was thrown away, the brushes soaked and cleaned and orders placed with his colour man for new materials.

Late one afternoon, Christos wandered into the kitchen as Angelica was preparing to leave at the end of her day. Sitting down at the table he said, "Angelica, I really am very grateful that you have helped me get this house back into good order. I also want to thank you for all the support you gave me during the time I was under the power of the blackness that enveloped me. I know I acted badly towards you and any sensible person would have walked away without a second thought and never returned but you didn't choose that, and I hope one day to repay the kindness you have shown me."

"It was nothing, Christos," Angelica replied.

Christos smiled and she smiled back, and they both knew a phase of their lives was over and a new one had arrived.

After a moment's pause, Christos said, "Tomorrow I would like to start drawing you, I feel ready to create again, so if you arrive at say ten in the morning we could begin."

When a while later Angelica left to go home, Christos walked with her to the door and took her hand, gently squeezing it. Looking in her eyes, he said, "I look forward to seeing you tomorrow, I will do my best to create a painting that is worthy of you."

She smiled again and said, "I will see you tomorrow. Enjoy your evening."

Christos watched her walk away along the old stones worn by the feet of people over many centuries, and only when she had disappeared from sight, did he turn and close the heavy door behind him, but he felt no sadness.

He turned the key in the door and walked up the stairs to the studio in a measured and calm way, recognising all the endeavours everyone had made on this house at his instigation or more truthfully, he thought, the cloak's instigation. He looked around, not at anything in particular, just generally feeling the freshness that had been instilled into the room and indeed into the whole building.

In front of him was his easel, supporting the rectangle of canvas stretched tight on its wooden bearers and primed white. In the gradually fading light, it loomed larger than its true proportions. To the table on his left, he had laid out jars of freshly made paint, along with some very old and some brand-new brushes, all clean and soft to the touch. Alongside them, there was turpentine, clean rags, his palette, a maulstick, which for fine work he had started to use now as his hand was less steady than in his youth, and a small box of sanguine coloured chalks. All he needed was assembled.

After eating some rice and peas which Angelica had made earlier, he returned to his rooms and after reading for a while, he took up his pen and wrote a few lines.

Breathe your fire into me,
Warm the coals of my being,
Show me the signs of the universe,
Let me know the laws of this world and be my guide,
Till we reach the light.

He looked at what he had written with detachment as if the words were not of his writing, not of his doing, and then with a half-smile, laid the paper aside, undressed and got into his bed. His head feeling heavy, he settled into the pillows, and as the final act of the day adjusted the cloak, which he once again had taken to laying across himself, and went to sleep.

Christos half-awoke in the night, whether from the moonlight, the thoughts of starting painting again in the morning, or just a creak in the fabric of the old house he didn't know, but the cloak was addressing him again in its calm way.

"Since we last spoke a lot has happened and I will tell you what you have done," the cloak said. "You opened your windows, you let in the sunlight, you got rid of all that which was old and worn and of no use. You cleaned the space you inhabit and you resolved to use the skills you have again.

"These things any man can see, but I know you have done these things to your inner self also and the result is the black monster you believed had you in its power, under its control, has not been seen. It has gone, has it not? That terrible spectre has left your life because you opened yourself up to the world. Although you were frightened of what the world had in store for you, to your surprise, there was no fear, and for you, only good things have happened.

"Now that you have taken those first steps, you have changed your blackness for light, and the negative viewpoint you had for a positive one, and I think you cannot but agree that your life is now immeasurably better. What you will do next is open up your life, your being, your spirit, your essence whatever you call it even more, for as you have found there is nothing to lose, nothing to fear in opening yourself up, and only warmth, light, and inner peace will come your way. It seems a good exchange, do you not think?

"Next, this is what I want you to do. You are going to start putting right the things you have done wrong. You may think this an impossible task as over the years those acts that went against the person you really are have become numerous, as they do with most of us, but remember you have me to help you.

"You probably recall in the linear sense of your history, the major events that even then you probably knew were against the path you should have been following. Then of course, there were the many forgotten actions you took, a small deception here, a harmful thought there, or a look that wished to cause some sort of harm, all these small instances we forget but even they can be undone and replaced with something good as you will see."

Christos' eyelids flickered as if responding to what he was hearing.

"Finally before I go and let you sleep some more, I am going to explain what happened to you during your time of darkness which you may think of as a time of loss and waste, but in a perverse way it was a time that saved you, so let me explain.

"Because of the material success and accolades you received when you were at the height of your career, which I grant were merited, you lost sight of the person you really are and pulled within yourself many negative and harmful attitudes because you thought only of the external, of the fortune you were amassing, and of the praise you were receiving from almost everyone you met. It all acted upon you as if you had swallowed poison every day, until, as you know, Christos, you sought ways of ending this time on earth.

"But now, as a result of the black vortex you were sucked into, due in part to the erosion of your life as it had been, all of those negative traits and characteristics have gone from you. Like the energy and strength gone from a mariner washed up on a distant shore, whose ship lies breaking on jagged rocks, and with it, gone the likelihood of him returning to the world he knew.

"So you are going to show, and be, from now on, temperate and restrained, charitable and giving. You will show composure and forgiveness, be kind and show admiration, retain purity in your thoughts, apply diligence, integrity and labour in your efforts, and above all, have humility wherever you go.

"Now sleep, daybreak is just two hours below the horizon and tomorrow Angelica will be here, on what for her will be one of the most special days of her life, and maybe for you too."

Just one chime rang out as the bell of the nearby church struck nine-thirty, but in the clear air, its sound entered the open windows of Christos' rooms with perfect clarity as if he was there in the church itself.

He had dressed and washed some time ago, with the thoughts of what the cloak had said to him playing across his mind, and those thoughts gave a feeling of tranquillity. That feeling of ease stayed with him through his breakfast, which was fresh water from a spring in the hills behind the city, which was collected daily by a local man in two large vats mounted on his cart, a pear, some cheese that seemed bluer than when Angelica had bought it back from the market a few days past, and two slices of rye bread.

With a half-hour to go before Angelica was due to arrive, Christos went and stood in the rectangle of his studio and looking around, checking everything was as he wanted it; it was.

Angelica arrived ten minutes early. Christos heard the waterside door open and went out onto the landing at the top of the stairs. He watched with a degree of amusement as Angelica in a slight state of irritation shook her blue headscarf, removing rainwater from the rain she had got caught in. Then aware she was not alone, Angelica looked up to see Christos smiling at her.

"What's wrong?" he said, knowing exactly what was wrong.

"Oh I got caught in an unexpected shower and the damp and this scarf have flattened my hair."

Going down the stairs and taking her coat from her, he said, "But you look lovely," then holding her hand, he led her back up to the studio.

After some hot tea which removed Angelica's sense of irritation at getting wet, he positioned her in a comfortable chair behind and slightly to the right of his easel and taking a piece of chalk, began to draw.

He did not talk much but she felt quite at ease as if the whole situation was not unusual. Just before one o'clock, he put down his chalk and asked if she would like to see what he had done; so with a degree of trepidation, she stood beside him at the easel.

On viewing the drawing, she felt a slight shock at what she saw. The likeness which Christos had portrayed was truly her, but she was surprised, as when one catches an unexpected glimpse of one's self in a mirror and you recognise yourself but you ask, is that me?

With not much food in the house, they walked to the bar where Christos had met the Arab some days earlier. After passing a pleasant hour they returned to recommence.

The afternoon for both passed quickly, and when the church bell rang five times Christos said, "That is enough for today, Angelica, we will continue tomorrow but before you go, may I ask a favour of you?"

"Yes, of course, Christos, what is it?"

"May I walk you home?"

As so often before, colour rose in her cheeks, "Thank you, I would like that," she said.

They closed the large front door of the house behind them and then turned left, away from the city's centre. Christos knew this area well as it led to the market, but then they turned left down an alleyway before they reached the market and here he became less familiar.

After another five minutes of twisting alleyways, Christos was completely unsure of his whereabouts but he did not mind. A while later they arrived in a small square enclosed on all sides by three-story buildings that almost seemed to be falling into the square they were crossing.

Outside a faded blue door, Angelica stopped. "This is where I live," she said, "I want to thank you for a very special and wonderful day and I look forward to tomorrow." Then with a quick movement, she kissed Christos on the cheek and disappeared through the door before he had a moment to react.

He looked at the door then at the ground he was standing on and for several moments he kept his head bowed. Then blinking, he returned to the present and started re-crossing the small square, but now it seemed different.

It was full of people jostling and calling out, moving this way and that carrying bundles, a man pushing a hand cart, two dogs snapping at each other, a lady with a large bosom and yellow hair selling fruit off a barrow and amongst all this, were children, some running in groups or some standing on their own.

Why he had been oblivious before he did not know, but as he watched the melee surrounding him, he noticed the children had no shoes, the man pushing the hand cart dragged one foot behind him, and the woman selling the fruit had patches on her dress.

Then a small girl with a smutty face grabbed his hand in an almost vicious way and asked for a coin or two. On seeing he did not pull away, other children came up to him with the same requests, but he was not carrying much change, so going over to the lady with the fruit stall he gave her a silver coin and said, "I will buy all you have."

She looked inquisitively at him and then at the coin and with a smile she said, "It is all yours."

With the children still around him he started giving out the fruit till it was all gone, he got no thanks but that was alright for they were all intent on eating.

After getting lost in the alleyways for a short while, he arrived home an hour later, and as the cloak had said, it had been a special day.

Just before dawn, the cloak visited Christos again. "It was a good day for you yesterday," it began. "You created something, you made Angelica feel unique and special, and you made the lives better, if only for a while, of the woman selling the fruit and the children you gave it to.

"What did it all cost you? A little bit of effort, some kind words and one silver coin. What you did yesterday is how you protect yourself from suffering as you have suffered, so you stop suffering by giving and saving others from the fears and darkness you so recently encountered.

"Helping others is the most important thing, more important than anything else, and if you keep giving, without expecting reward, all your wishes for happiness will come true and good things will come to you.

"It is a universal law that every action done with a positive or negative mind has consequences as a result, so the choice is always yours. I know Christos which choice of action you will make and I am sure I do not need to tell you, but nevertheless I will. Every action in your life should be done with a good heart, without ignorance, without desire, without attachment, and the result, as you found yesterday, will be happiness."

That morning, Angelica again arrived a few minutes earlier than the tenth hour. Christos was not there to greet her, as the day before, but was in the studio with his back to the door, looking out of the window that overlooked the courtyard.

Upon hearing her enter, he turned and smiled and going over to the table gave her a bouquet of flowers he had bought from the market just after dawn. He kissed her on the cheek while gently holding her forearms as Angelica let her body press against his chest.

"Thank you for the flowers, they are beautiful," she said. Breaking his tender grip, she turned and went to the kitchen for a vase.

The morning's drawing went well and they were both happy in each other's company. Christos recounted to her the events that happened in the square after leaving her, and Angelica told him that not only his presence with her but also his actions had created a lot of gossip and talk amongst her neighbours.

They stayed at Moon Street for their midday meal, eating foods Angelica had bought in with her, bread, cheese, ham, and strawberries which she covered in sugar, while Christos produced a bottle of sweet dark yellow wine from the storeroom on the ground floor.

As they ate, they talked of the morning's work. Christos felt pleased with what had been done so far and thought that probably tomorrow or perhaps the day after, he would start using paint. He explained how he would start by applying some broad areas of colour to the background aiming to catch the quality of light that fell into the room and lit her in such a subtle way.

Although she already knew because she had witnessed it so many times before, she let him speak so as not to dampen his enthusiasm and excitement. She watched him with a relaxed smile. He had not seemed so animated for a long time, his hands, with their pronounced veins and long fingers, gesticulating, emphasising words and thoughts, and describing shapes and forms in the still afternoon light, which was flecked through with minute particles of dust that he cut through with invisible incisions.

She watched his eyes, were they a soft grey, blue or green? It did not matter which, as they changed in appearance almost with the moment. After the torments she had seen him go through, she was just filled with happiness, both for him and herself, and as his eyes sparkled, she saw herself in her best green dress reflected in them.

"I am very pleased for you," she said when his bubbling of emotion paused slightly and the vacuum of no words arrived, and in the silence, they were content with each other.

After a moment or two, Christos said, "I want you to know all about me Angelica, it has for me become the most important thing I want to do. You see I realise I have great affection for you, more than for anyone I have ever known, and maybe if I tell you about me, you might feel that way too."

Angelica smiled saying, "Christos you have no need to tell me anything, but anything you say will be a pleasure to hear."

"Then I will start by telling you this, it concerns a gift I was given. You probably recall that when I first arrived from the countryside, a youth unknowing of almost everything, Master Paulo gave me simple tasks both here in the studio and the outside world."

Angelica nodded.

"One of those tasks was to collect the food from the market, and when I did that, the last stall I always called at was run by an old lady called Antonina who sold the bread. I used to get such a good and warm feeling from her so I saved seeing her till last, you probably remember her too."

Angelica smiled, recalling the old bread woman.

"Well after getting the bread there a few times, one day she said she had something for me and gave me a parcel which I brought back here to unwrap. In it was a cloak, a dark blue cloak with coloured patterns and designs on the front of it, did anyone ever tell you about it?"

"No, I have never heard anyone mention it," she replied.

"I suppose the only person who did know, was Stuardo," Christos said, "And the poor fellow could not utter a word. I laid the cloak across my bed as it got very cold in the attic, but as well as keeping me warm, it gave me wonderful dreams, and the boyhood dream I had of becoming an artist, started to come true.

Angelica listened, wide-eyed.

As you know, I became the most renowned and respected artist in the whole of Europe. But the fame, wealth, and adulation, changed me into a person no one should become. Then when the old duke died, my material life crumbled, and as you know I shut myself away from the world and reached a point when I did not want to see another dawn.

She felt saddened, knowing how close Christos had come to ending his life.

"Then one night the cloak spoke to me and has done several times since, it told me what I must do and I listened and heeded its advice. Since then my life has improved beyond all measure and the most tangible, the most important change, is I have you, Angelica, to be with and hopefully, to know for the rest of my days."

Laying his hand on the table in a gesture of offering, she took it and held it tightly.

"May I see this cloak?" Angelica said.

"Of course," Christos replied. "It is across my bed, I will show you," and they made their way up the wooden staircase to Christos' rooms.

The light of the day was fading so Christos took a tinderbox from the table and lit several lamps, creating a warm yellow glow throughout the rooms.

"There it is," he said gesturing at his bed, "My cloak."

Angelica sat down on the edge of the bed and touched the cloth with gentle reverence, the dark blue of the cloak seemed almost black in the lamplight and the beads that interspersed the strange patterns reflected the light, making it seem ethereal and unworldly.

"It is simply beautiful," she said.

They talked some more, she sitting on the bed, he in a chair and the time passed. Then with the sound of the church bell, they realised it had become late but still they talked on.

Their words became less and Angelica, tired, moved back onto the bed and settled into the pillows saying it was probably the wine. Then closing her eyes, she fell asleep.

Christos watched silently and seeing she was in a deep sleep, eased the cloak and covers from under her, removed her shoes and gently holding her feet, put them under the bedding. Then he pulled the cover and cloak back over her body and put out all but one of the lamps. He sat back down in his chair and simply watched her breathe.

~ Chapter Seventeen ~

The sounds of nothing in particular woke her, it could have been the flap of a bird's wing going by the window, the creak maybe of masts and rigging on a boat in the harbour, perhaps a splash of sunlight across her eyelids, or just a thought crossing her mind that morning had arrived.

There was no disorientation on waking as to where she was. As she stretched slightly, feeling happy, she turned on her side and watched Christos, crumpled, asleep still in the chair, but although the years had lined his face, the young man who had first arrived at Moon Street with his dream was there revealed, and she wanted to look after him and stay with him for as long as possible.

She rose and padded across the ornate carpet, washed, arranged her hair as best she could, retrieved her shoes from the bedroom and went and prepared a breakfast of scrambled eggs and herb tea.

She took it back upstairs and placing it down on a low table gently shook Christos on the shoulder till he woke.

"Breakfast," she said.

"Thank you, I am so pleased you are here," he said.

After breakfast, they walked to the quayside, then on around to the rocky promontory that gave the natural harbour a horseshoe shape.

"I have been thinking," he said, as they walked with a slow leisurely pace, "about the people I saw in your square, especially the children. You know for an artist who depends entirely on his sight, I have been blind to so many things. I have more money hidden away than would last me ten lifetimes, so with your help, I want to try and improve the lot of those that have so little but I am not sure how to go about it. I could simply give it all away but very soon it would have all been spent and my efforts would have been short-lived, making no lasting change."

Holding hands they walked on, Christos with his head lowered, deep in thought.

After a while, Angelica spoke.

"The little church in the square where I live has a wonderful priest called Father Roberto. His church is small and not frequented by the wealthy of this city, but with the help of other priests in similar circumstances they endeavour to feed and give shelter to as many as they can when the weather is bad but they lack the resources to do the work they would really like to do. Perhaps you could meet him and see if you could be of assistance?"

"That is a wonderful idea, Angelica, we, if you will accompany me, will call on him later in the day and find out if we can be of help."

Cheered by his plan of action, Christos kissed Angelica on the lips and the two returned to the studio at a quickened pace.

Christos started painting a little later than he had intended but the thought of assisting Father Roberto in his work with the poor and needy filled him with a sense of wellbeing and happiness, unlike anything he had known. Whether that was the cause or not, the background paint he applied worked first time as if his hand and touch were being guided by something outside of himself.

Later as they walked through the maze-like streets and alleyways to the church of Father Roberto, the Church of Saint Daphne, Christos said, "Angelica, I want you to be always with me, with you my life seems complete and I never want it again to be any other way, will you stay with me tonight and every other night to come?"

Angelica was quiet for some time and then said, "No, Christos, I cannot stay with you tonight, it would be wrong as we are not married, and as much as I wish to spend my life with you, I cannot do as you ask. It would go against all I believe. Also the status I have as a moral and honourable woman, if I lived with you in such a way, would disappear."

They walked on through the twists and turns of this quieter part of the city before entering an elongated square with six lime trees in three groups of two at its centre.

It was late afternoon and those that had work had not yet returned home, only an old woman with a bent back wearing a black dress that touched the ground could be seen carrying a bucket into a doorway on the far side.

The Church of Saint Daphne was to the right side of the rectangular square, it was not imposing, no higher than the three-storey narrow houses that adjoined it. At the entrance, it had three semi-circular steps worn down by many a foot and a door of dark wood that had been cut from a tree many years past whose lower edge was frayed by time and perhaps mice seeking sanctuary.

The space inside was quiet and the light diffused, entering through transoms high up on either side and from a small two-colour stained-glass window above the altar. There was also an unfortunate smell of damp.

Christos counted the rows of pews, twelve on either side of the nave, and if each one was taken, then about a hundred would be the maximum congregation.

Angelica crossed herself and bowed and Christos followed her example.

Seeing no one around, Christos said, "Where will we find Father Roberto?"

"I am not sure," Angelica replied, "But he lives in the house next door."

As they were turning to go back outside again, Father Roberto entered. He was younger than Christos had imagined, perhaps in his early thirties. Hispanic looking, being slightly on the short side for men of this city, but he was broad and muscular with a black beard and long curly hair. In his black cassock, he formed a large mass which seemed to block the light from the open doorway behind him, making it filter round him like an eclipse.

"Angelica, how lovely to see you," he said, his face breaking into one large smile. While gently holding her small hand, he quickly studied Christos' face, taking in every detail, crease, and line as if equating these worldly signs and divining from them the character of the man before him.

"It is an honour, sir, that you, Master Christos Azzuro, the most renowned artist in Europe, are here in my humble church and accompanying my good friend Angelica, who is one of my most devout worshippers."

Both Christos and Angelica were taken aback and slightly embarrassed by his comments but both saw his words were not flattery. Christos wondered how the priest knew him.

Father Roberto then asked, "Why are you both here, and in what way can I help you?"

The pair sat down on the pew at the back with Father Roberto on the one in front, his body turned, giving them his full attention.

Angelica spoke first, "As you already know, I am a maid, but you might not know that I worked for Master Benidicto and then upon his death for Master Christos." She continued, "Christos asked my advice this morning as to what he could do with his money, so I

173

suggested coming here to see if you would be interested in his aid with your work with the children and the poor."

Father Roberto listened intently and said. "Thank you, Angelica, for having me and my work in your thoughts, and of course, the more help we have the better. Your idea this morning is indeed very worthy and if you could assist in buying food or some basic clothing, then you would certainly help those who have next to nothing, especially the orphans whose mothers have been unable to cope and have been left on our steps."

Angelica was pleased to hear her idea would work.

"The mothers are mostly unknown to us but they do not give up hope of one day being able to be reunited with their children because the common practice is to leave half a torn playing card with the child and then if later in their life things should improve, they return presenting their half of the card as proof of who is their boy or girl. We then check the ledgers where the torn cards are kept and having satisfied ourselves that the woman is in a stable situation and with the wherewithal to support the child, return the boy or girl to her. Unfortunately, I have to tell you it happens very rarely."

Christos spoke for the first time, "Father Roberto, yes, I will indeed do these things you have mentioned but my idea was to help you in your work in a far more substantial way. Over the years of being an artist, I have amassed a small fortune which lies dormant, not serving any useful purpose, but today I have briefly mulled over what I would like to do with the wealth I have.

"My mother, although she had very little, and always worked hard, made sure I never went hungry and had shoes on my feet, and our modest house protected us from the changing seasons, and she taught me right from wrong and gave me love and affection. So I would like to fund and expand your orphanage and provide schooling for those less fortunate.

"Also during the next few days, I will go to the son of my erstwhile patron and friend, the young duke, and request that he invest my money for me and get his legal secretary Felix Rosa to draw up a deed of trust that will sustain your good works and the orphanage long after we are both gone from this place, what do you say, Father?"

"Christos, the offer you have made fulfils my every dream," he clasped the artist's hand and his face broke into a huge smile.

"There is something else," Christos said, "and this seems the right time and place." Turning to Angelica, he said, "Will you marry me?"

With only a moment's hesitation due to shock, she answered, "Of course I will, I have loved you for a long while."

With that, he held her delicate oval face and kissed her tenderly on the lips.

Father Roberto let out a generous laugh and congratulated them, "Can I assume you will marry here?"

Angelica nodded and smiled, too overcome to speak.

"Good, then I shall post the various notices, and as today is a Friday set the date for four weeks from tomorrow."

They walked the short distance from the church to Angelica's house, not saying a great deal, simply feeling warm inside that they were together.

At her door, she said, "You have made me happier than I have ever felt," and looking around to see if anyone was watching, kissed him on the cheek.

"I will see you tomorrow morning, Angelica. We have wedding plans to make and a painting to finish. Sweet dreams."

Christos walked home with a sense of youthfulness, oblivious of any passers-by, and as he walked, the familiar voice of the cloak spoke to him. "You trusted me and have turned your life around. You deserve to be happy."

Back in Moon Street, Christos made some tea, an infusion of rose syrup, hawthorn and lemon. Then going to the balcony above the waterfront door, he sat and reflected on his day, closing his eyes and letting the last warmth of the day play across his face. On the breeze, the sounds of a group of musicians practising somewhere drifted his way, a lute, a soprano voice, a viola perhaps and a flute.

With the tea drunk, he set to work starting in the entrance hall. As he had when he buried it, he took a sharp knife, inserting it between the edges of the flags, lifted it, scraped for a moment with the knife in the compacted earth and retrieved the green bag full of diamonds.

During the following hours, he worked his way through the entire house, retrieving his hidden wealth and just before midnight everything was there on the table in his room glittering in the lamplight.

He wrote down an inventory of what he had and placed it all in two large sacks from the storeroom before falling asleep.

~ Chapter Eighteen ~

Angelica arrived an hour early. She had already been to the market and had bought bread, olives, cheese, apples, figs and grapes.

As she was unpacking them, Christos came in and gently kissed her on the cheek. "Good morning, I have something to show you," he gestured to the two sacks sitting in the corner of the studio.

Slightly puzzled she turned to him.

"Look inside," he said, loosening the cord on one of the sacks and opening its top.

As she looked, she realised the fortune Christos had amassed as the sacks were packed to the brim with gold and silver coin and jewels of every colour.

With a smile, he said, "I think this will be ample to assist Father Roberto when it is properly invested. I will arrange to go and see the young duke and express my remorse at the arrogance and poor attitude I used to have in his presence, and ask him if, through his bankers, they will create a yearly income so that the orphanage grows and grows and will never be short of money again."

She sat and he painted till the midday bells rang. Then Christos stopped, with the portrait beginning to take shape. Over lunch, they discussed their wedding, who they would like to be there, and where the meal afterwards should be and they decided it should be here in Moon Street.

Christos then said, "I will arrange for a dressmaker to call on you tomorrow to measure you for your wedding dress. She is very good. Her name is Maria, she only has one eye, the other is glass, and she's married to a tailor I used to use. This morning I also sent word to ask for an appointment with the duke, so hopefully, I will hear back soon. As to who will give you away, since your dear father is long dead, I thought that Claudio Mondino the physician would be a good choice as I know he is very fond of you."

"If he accepts," Angelica said, "I would feel very happy."

After they had eaten and before resuming the afternoon sitting, they took a short walk. They did not say anything to each other for neither felt the need, they just moved along the quayside feeling almost invisible to those they passed.

The sun danced on the water, making it sparkle like a million diamonds, the breeze gently blew from the south, and the dark days that had been Christos' world until recently seemed to belong to someone else.

On their return, standing outside the door, stood a page dressed in the livery of the duke.

"Have you something for me?" Christos asked as they approached.

"Are you Christos Azzuro?" the page replied.

While turning the key in the front door Christos nodded in affirmation and the page handed him a blue rectangular envelope embossed with the Castello seal.

Standing in the hallway, he slipped his thumb into the slight opening of the envelope which the seal had not held down tightly and with a little pressure broke the wax. The ink on the letter was black and the script scrawling, but after a moment or two, Christos deciphered what it said and read it to Angelica.

"Dear Christos Azzuro, the duke wishes me to inform you that he is engaged with duties of the court for the next three days but has set aside the hours between ten and noon on Monday and looks forward to your visit. Signed Chief Secretary to the Duke of Castello, Felix Rosa."

"I know that man," Christos said. "I have met him a few times. He was the old duke's lawyer, and I see he has risen in status since that time. He is a very able man. You do understand, Angelica, that I shall have to go alone to see the duke and I may find it a difficult meeting."

"Of course," she replied and squeezed his hand in reassurance.

They resumed the portrait, with Angelica resting her arms on the marks that Christos had painted on the chair so that she was in virtually the same position as every time before. Then she quarter-turned her head and looked to the window, and Christos knew that by the time the light had faded he would have captured her image in the way wanted.

Later he walked her home and while holding her hand said. "You know, Angelica, you have restored the energy in me. As you know, until very recently I had none, and no hope of a good future, or in fact, any future at all, and if there are such things as miracles, then one has happened to me and it was your love and patience that created it."

When they stopped at her door he said, "Tonight I am going to paint and finish our picture. I know what I intend and I will work till dawn if necessary."

Then kissing her lightly on the cheek, he said goodnight.

Back at Moon Street, Christos collected as many lamps as he had to light the studio as brightly as possible. The background which until now he had left vague, he decided would in some way be a depiction of the journey he had made all those years ago from the house he had shared with his mother.

He painted in pale distant blues and greens, the land where he had tended the chickens and watered the vegetables. He remembered the track he had followed when leaving, and where he had stood on top of the hill and seen the village where his life had started, now just a speck in the distance.

As he painted, he recalled the pieces of charcoal and the lumps of red earth he had first used to draw with. He recalled the meadows of wildflowers, the trees bent by the winds, and the huge clouds that, in his youth, seemed so vast, scudding across the dome of the sky under which he lived his simple plain life that was made wondrous by what he saw. At that time, he had felt those skies were his alone.

His thoughts turned to the moment when he took a few steps over the crest of the hill so that his home where he was born was no longer visible. Forever to be but a memory, and like all memories, shaped by the passing of time, so that its true reality was changed and coloured by everything that came after.

This gave him a sadness because he did not want to forget how it was, and the smoky greys, blues, violets and greens that he used for that distant background were exactly right for the feelings of that place and time.

Below the range of distant hills, he painted a track leading to a small village and the colour he used became stronger. He remembered the boys playing their game with glass balls on the dusty ground and wondered if they still lived there, maybe now perhaps with sons or daughters of their own, and the innkeeper, was he still alive? Sadly maybe not, and he thought of the meeting with Giorgio, who literally put him on the road to where he was now and wondered what had become of him.

Oblivious of the hour, he painted on, and as he was completing painting the walls around the city he now lived in, the first hint of the new day showed itself through the window.

Laying down his brushes, a sense tranquillity came over him, both for the finishing of the picture and because it was the first painting he had done since he had arrived in this place that was for himself and not for financial reward.

Angelica woke him with a kiss. He was slumped with his head tilted sideways onto his shoulder and with his legs splayed out in the chair she had used to pose in.

As he woke, he pulled his limbs together, smiled and said, "It's almost finished, just the two dots of reflected light in your eyes to do and I am pleased. I am very pleased."

Looking at the painting on the easel in front of him, she said, "It is beautiful, Christos," and she fought to hold back the emotion she felt.

Sensing her reflective mood and not wishing so early in the day to join her in those sentiments, and somehow feeling slightly and strangely embarrassed at the beauty of his painting, he changed the subject. "We have a visitor coming for lunch, Physician Mondino, it is a long time since we have seen him and I want to ask him if he will give you away. As he likes your food so much, could you prepare something special?"

"This is short notice," she said, but after a moment's thought, "I would love to but I will need your help. You will have to go to the market and get me the following, three fresh fish, fennel, sweet potatoes, tomatoes, a strong blue cheese – it should be ripe, two wheat loaves, three bottles of wine, one red, one white, and one sweet, also green walnuts if you can find them, six pears, oh and another bottle of white wine so that is four, and two bunches of black grapes." She said with a smile, "And be as quick as you can."

Mondino arrived slightly early and he still bounded into the house as if he was thirty years younger than he was. The meal was a great success with the dessert of pears steeped in white wine bringing raptures of praise from the physician.

During the meal, Christos told the physician of his life since they had last met, and of how Angelica had stood steadfastly by him. Then how he came to realise he loved her and wished to spend the rest of his days with her. He explained her circumstance of having no one to give her away at their wedding and that they both were hoping that he would do them that honour.

Mondino bowed his head and appeared quite solemn. "On one condition," he said, "which is, that I can eat here more often," and burst out laughing.

Standing up, he held Angelica to him and kissing her heartily on both cheeks, said, "I will be delighted to give you away, my dear. You are a beautiful woman and I already think of you as my daughter."

On the morning of the meeting with the duke, Christos walked through the streets, alleys and squares feeling no fear or trepidation about seeing the duke again after all these months. In fact, fear of what lay ahead had, he realised, left him some time past. Now there were only possibilities for the future, but perhaps for the first time, he was aware of it.

He presented his letter to the guard at the top of the steps who beckoned a page to escort him. They walked through the great hall, a place of so many memories. Servants were walking back and forth with table linen, cutlery, glasses, and flowers preparing for some forthcoming banquet and entering and leaving by the many doors set into the room's panelling. Then in the far corner, he caught sight of

Zona giving instructions to four young maids.

"One moment," he said to the page who was walking in front of him, and he went over to the group of women. "May I have a moment of your time?" he said addressing Zona.

She turned and looked at him and in the instant of recognising him, dismissed the maids to their tasks.

"I am sorry," he said. "I wish to apologise for my behaviour that night and although I do not expect you to forgive me, I am a changed person, and who I am today will carry the weight of my past actions forevermore."

Her face gave no indication of her feelings as she spoke. "I am married, as perhaps you know, and have a child who gives me much joy and I am content with my life. I recall the evening you refer to but long since any malice I had for you, I removed from my life. Holding on to such feelings would have been like carrying poison within me every day so I forgave you, as much for my sake as yours."

Christos, humbled by the woman's dignity, bowed ever so slightly and said, "Thank you. I wish you a happy life."

She briefly closed her eyes in acknowledgement.

Christos re-joined the page who seemed annoyed at having to pause and wait but said nothing as he knocked on the library door, the room where Christos had last seen his friend, the old duke.

A voice from inside told them to enter and there was Felix Rosa surrounded by papers. He looked up and smiled warmly.

Christos was at first slightly surprised not to find the duke but also at how much older the lawyer now seemed. His eyes, magnified by the thick-lensed glasses he wore, seemed to bulge as would a frog's but he was a kindly man and he was very pleased to see him. "Felix, good morning, how are you? It has been a while."

Felix, who always liked to talk, started to relay almost every detail of his life since they last met. Then, after some time, he brought his words round to the reason for Christos being there.

He said, "I can invest all the fortune you have amassed in exactly the way I do for the duke and every year he shows a marked interest on his capital.

"Your precious artefacts and jewellery we could sell on the open market but I suggest, for the present, you deposit them for safekeeping in the royal vaults and we can perhaps look for specialised dealers in such things in the future.

"Then from what you have intimated, your wealth should generate enough income for ten orphanages and I will call upon you as soon as possible to take a full inventory."

Christos marvelled that his wealth could do so much good.

"Also the duke has told me that all fees to us will be waived as a gesture of goodwill for your past work for his family, and also because of the noble and generous deed you are undertaking."

At that point, the young duke entered and both men stood. "Christos, Felix, please sit," he said. "Word has it that you have been through a challenging time of late and those here in the court that know you are pleased and happy that it seems to be over."

"You seem to know a lot about my recent life," Christos replied.

"Like it or not, I hear of virtually everything that happens in this city, and as you are one of its most illustrious citizens, of you I have heard more than most."

"I see," said Christos, slightly taken aback. "But if I may, I would like to tell you why I wished to see you today."

"Of course," replied the duke, "Please tell."

"After your father's death, I felt I behaved in a discourteous and arrogant way to you, for which I would like to apologise."

"Apology accepted, Christos, I too at that time behaved in a less than noble way to you and many others besides, but that time is now behind us. Nevertheless, there is one favour I would ask of you."

"Certainly, what is it?"

"I would like to be invited to your wedding."

"It would be a great honour," Christos replied standing and shaking the duke's hand.

"Thank you," said the duke. "I will get Felix here to call on you tomorrow. I would also like to assist in making your day as special as possible, if you and your bride Angelica agree."

The following day Angelica arrived with flowers from the market and while she arranged them, Christos told her of his meeting with the duke.

After a few moments thought, she said, "Christos, I hold no one responsible but I have a slight degree of concern that our special day will be turned into something close to a state occasion with the duke, his wife, and all the other court dignitaries attending. It seems impossible to reject his offer; indeed I feel very honoured that a woman such as myself should have such a prestigious wedding."

As Christos listened to Angelica, there was a knock on the front door. It was Felix who had arrived by royal barge which waited at the waterfront mooring.

"I am so sorry I am late but we had to stop as two small boats collided and we went to their assistance, fortunately no one was hurt but one boat lost three sacks of grain. Still the fishes will feed well."

Felix did not seem a romantic or poetic man but at the sight of Angelica's portrait on the easel, this garrulous man fell into what appeared to be awe and simply said, "It is beautiful."

When Angelica herself entered the room, he took her hand and kissed it, then gathering himself for the purpose of his visit, he produced a green leather ledger from his bag on the floor, along with a bottle of black ink and a quill pen, stating, "Shall we begin?"

Christos and Felix sat for nearly three hours counting the coins, then writing in duplicate what was there, and finally putting the coin in yellow bags marked with the Castello insignia.

When they had finished and been refreshed with a vegetable and rice dish, Felix signed and put a seal on a copy of the inventory which he gave to Christos, then got two of the men from the waiting barge to collect the sacks and carry it back on board.

Thanking Angelica at the doorway for the meal and hospitality, he also informed Christos that after thirty days, the interest gained from the money, soon to be under the duke's safekeeping, would create income for his project with Father Roberto and more besides.

With that, he bowed and went aboard the waiting barge.

Christos felt a sense of relief with his amassed wealth now in the safekeeping of the House of Castello, the burden of which he seemed to have carried for a long time.

When Felix had gone, they were both rather quiet, keeping their thoughts to themselves but Christos spoke first. "What is wrong Angelica? You seem worried, is it because the duke wishes to be at our wedding?"

"Yes, I suppose the special day of our wedding, which I wanted as a simple affair seems to be becoming too grand. I know you are famous and, as was shown only a moment ago, very wealthy, but these were not the reasons I wanted to be your wife. I want to be your wife because I love you and want to share the rest of my days with you."

"I love you too and feel the same," Christos replied.

"I suppose things changed when the duke asked to be invited. It is a great honour, as I have said, for a simple maid as myself to be married in the presence of someone so illustrious but it has moved our day away from what I thought it was going to be."

"He is just a man, Angelica, but yes he does carry with him the splendour of court and I am not sure how I can redress the situation."

He walked to the window and without focus, watched the people going about their daily lives, carrying bundles, standing in small groups talking, two young women walking, one in blue the other in yellow and a sailor worse for wear weaving his way somewhere.

As he watched, his thoughts went back to that afternoon when he had walked Angelica home. When he had become aware of the children with no shoes, the old man with the damaged leg, and the woman selling fruit, wearing a dress that was patched and held together with threads.

Turning away from the window, he said, "Maybe I have a solution, it is not the duke's wedding, it is ours. So I suggest we open our day to all your neighbours and all those that live in that square. Of course, they cannot all be inside the church as there is not room. But if we leave its doors open, they can share our day and the rich will have to share with the poor, the grand mix with the humble, and instead of having a reception here we will hold it in the square itself. If you recall, the duke said he would assist us in any manner that we needed, so he can provide all the food, wine and ale, musicians and other entertainers, and give those people you have lived amongst a day and evening that will live long in their memories. What do you say?"

"You have cheered me enormously. It is a splendid idea." Getting up, she walked over to him and gave him a big kiss.

"I must return home now," she said, "And I will not see you tomorrow as your dressmaker is calling again for a final fitting."

Christos replied, "Then I will go to the palace and put forward our plans."

Christos met Felix in his rooms on the first floor of the palace and as the day was warm and sultry, they went into the gardens and sat amongst the scented shrubs near a fountain while Christos explained his ideas for the wedding.

"Yes I can attend to it all," Felix said. "I will send the court surveyor to measure the square, and he will draw up a plan of what will go where and how it will be transported. Master Carlucci, the man with the golden hat you may remember from the banquets, who is in charge of all festivities, will accompany him to see where we should erect the dais for the musicians and so on. All I will require of you is a list of the guests you wish to have in the church, and also to stay away from the square the three days before the wedding."

"Thank you, Felix. You are invited of course."

"I shall bring my wife, thank you, my friend."

Christos was in a good mood and walked home with energy bubbling inside him. It was such a good feeling, and he realised he was smiling.

"You see!" a voice said in his mind.

Christos let out a laugh. It caught the attention of a couple passing by who looked at him as though there was something wrong with his state of mind, which made him laugh again.

At his door in Moon Street, he felt for his keys but then let them slip back into the depths of his pocket and carried on walking.

Ten or so minutes later, he was in the square of Saint Daphne and looking around, he envisaged the scene that would fill this space when he married Angelica.

He walked up the church steps, adding a degree of erosion to their stone, and quietly opened wide the old doors.

Two women were kneeling in prayer, one on the right at the rear, and one on the left closer to the front. The air was cool in the subdued light and the hubbub of the streets gone. As the still moments passed, he recalled the splendours of the cathedral which contrasted to the pared-down space he was in and he knew that grand decoration, gilding, rich fabrics and expensive coloured glass made no difference. If anything, they acted as a distraction from the essence of the building which was the simple idea of reflection, contemplation, and compassion.

The voice of a woman carrying a vase of lilies coming out of a side door near the altar caught his ear and looking up, he saw she was talking to Father Roberto.

When she had gone, Christos stood and walked down the side aisle. "Father?" he quietly called out, and the large frame of Roberto turned towards him.

"Christos, how good to see you, how have you been?"

"I am well," Christos replied, "but I need a bit of your time."

The pair sat down on the front pew.

"I have some important news to tell you. Since our last meeting, I have been to the palace and met with the duke, and although you did not know of our disagreements, our differences are now behind us, so much so, that he has requested that he be a guest at my wedding."

Father Roberto's eyebrows raised and his mouth half-fell open in surprise.

"This of course, alters the status of the occasion," Christos continued. "And this, in some ways, I regret, but it is also a great honour for Angelica and myself. As a result, we have changed the place of the celebrations afterwards, we are going to have it right here in the square and everyone from roundabout will be welcome.

Father Roberto listened in surprise.

"Everything will be provided by the palace. Soon a Felix Rosa will call upon you and with your assistance, will make all the necessary arrangements. He is also the man who will oversee the investment of my money and he informs me that in around a month the first amount of funds should be available to you for help with the orphanage and hopefully then the school."

"All this is wonderful, Christos, our meeting has been serendipitous and is going to change the lives of so many for the better."

"There is one final thing, Father. Have you a measure?"

"Yes, there is one in the vestry, why?"

"Because if you wish it, I will paint an altarpiece for you. At present, I have no work to occupy me and it would give me great pleasure to create such a thing during the coming months."

"Your generosity, Christos, has given me one of the best days of my life." With that, he wrapped his bear-like arms around Christos and gave him a hug.

~ Chapter Nineteen ~

On leaving the church, he walked to Angelica's house and was about to knock on her door as it opened and Maria the dressmaker with the glass eye appeared.

"How is the dress progressing?" he asked.

"It is all done, sir, and your lady looks wonderful."

"What colour is it, may I ask?"

"I cannot tell you that, sir, it would be bad fortune for me to do so or for you to see it but I can tell you it is the most exquisite garment I have ever made."

With that, she nodded slightly and with her large tapestry bag under her arm, went on her way. The door was still ajar and Christos knocked, as he did not wish to cross the threshold.

"Maria is that you, have you forgotten something?" Angelica appeared at the door.

"Christos how lovely to see you. Maria the seamstress has just left. I thought it was her. She has created a dress I could only dream of."

"I am so glad. I was with Father Roberto making final arrangements and I wanted to see you because, from tomorrow, it will be seven days till our wedding and custom frowns on me seeing you until then."

"I know," she said, "But from next week, we can spend every moment together." Then she kissed him quickly on the cheek, smiled while holding his fingers and said, "Now go."

Before going home, Christos detoured through the alleyways to his paint merchant's house. Daylight was almost gone and in the square, the lights were being lit, illuminating women preparing evening meals with their voices and those of their families reverberating in the air. The merchant's wife, now old but still with an elegance that would never leave her, answered the door.

"Master Christos, what a pleasant surprise. Please come in, we are just about to eat, join us."

"I am sorry to impose upon you at this hour, but it smells very good, so thank you."

On entering the small room, Christos saw the merchant with a bowl of steaming stew and vegetables in front of him.

"Ah Christos, what brings you here?"

No sooner had he sat down and answered than a dish identical to the merchant's was placed in front of him.

"My visit is twofold, one to invite you both to my wedding," he smiled at the merchant's wife. "And two, I need a wooden panel as quickly as you are able, delivered to my studio."

"The panel my nephew will commence work on tomorrow and should be with you in a matter of days and as for the wedding, we will be delighted."

On Sunday, Christos started doing preparatory sketches of the painting for the church, the idea of which was quite simple. Using chiaroscuro modelling, he would depict a blind man regaining his sight by receiving inner light and understanding from his spiritual teacher and so becoming conscious and aware.

He liked the idea the more he worked on it, and in his mind's eye, he could already see the contrasts between the black and earth tones against the whites, yellows, pale blues and pinks.

On Monday, he had two visitors, the first was the goldsmith with the wedding rings. They were both simple bands, not too wide, and he'd had them inscribed with a rectangle inside of which were an A and a C overlapped. He was pleased with the result, paid and thanked the man.

His second visitor, late in the afternoon, was the merchant's nephew accompanied by a friend. They delivered the wooden panel he had requested only a few days before wrapped in hessian to keep it protected, which they carefully placed against the studio wall.

Although the city made the best canvas that could be found because of the sails needed for the fleets of ships that sailed out of it, Christos had decided to paint on wood.

The panel was made of three pieces of poplar wood joined and sanded, it had then been sized by covering it with fine linen, stuck on with animal glue, and then covered in gesso, a mixture of chalk, more rabbit skin glue and white pigment, and each successive layer had been smoothed so that the finished result was a hard marble-like surface.

When they had gone, he ran his hand across its surface with a sort of reverence, and with the idea of what he was going to paint already fixed in his thoughts, he traced out with his fingers where each part would be, the master, the blind man, the landscape revealing itself behind their forms, the areas that would be almost as dark as night, and finally the parts that would be imbued with light. He felt good and complete by the task that lay before him.

On Tuesday, he rose later than usual and wondered what Angelica was doing. Going to the window, he saw the sky was full of clouds, in different greys, from almost black like the smoke after a cannon fires, to fluffy white clouds, big and soaring up to the very reaches of the dome. He decided to walk for a while, eat in the bar where he had spoken to the Arab and then come back and draw.

Across the city, in his rooms on the third floor of the palace, Felix awoke not knowing his wife had gently nudged him.

Later he went down to his office and told a page to ask Master Carlucci and Fra Paciolli the surveyor to join him in forty minutes, or sooner if possible.

Carlucci arrived first, then arriving late as he nearly always did, which Felix always thought odd for a man of precision and exactitude, was the surveyor Fra Paciolli with, of course, his assistant Luca in attendance.

They knew of their reason for being there, having been told over dinner the night before. Having gathered all they needed, they made the journey across the city as far as they could by barge then walked the rest of the way, with Luca bringing up the rear, carrying Fra Paciolli's instruments.

Fra Paciolli and Luca, with the aid of a ball of yellow twine that was tied with evenly spaced knots and three striped poles, measured and mapped the dimensions of the square and noted it down in a small brown book.

Master Carlucci did not do much but simply looked and walked around the square while Felix went and found Father Roberto and introduced himself, explaining what his colleagues were doing.

Those that lived in the square had never seen such interest in where they lived and the children with no sense of shyness or reserve went up to the four men and wanted to know who they were and why they were there. A couple slyly looked in the surveyor's bag until Luca shooed them away.

After an hour, they had done what they wanted and said their goodbyes. Then back on the barge, they discussed their ideas and agreed to meet later that afternoon to finalise what they were going to do.

Fra Paciolli laid out his drawing of the rectangular square on the table; the map showed the six lime trees, along with the position of the church and the four alleyways which were roughly in each corner.

"We need the stage there," said Master Carlucci, pointing at the plan.

"And I suggest we have the spit roast as far away from the church doors as possible," said Felix Rosa. "To make the best use of the space, we should have the trestles serving food mostly on the south-western side. With a few more, if needed, on the north-western side, here and here," indicating their position with a short stubby finger. He added, "We also need tables for people to sit at to eat or if they become tired."

Then after some more wine, they drew up a list of what was needed to be dispatched, then spent the rest of the evening telling each other stories.

Three barges left the palace the following day loaded with wood, awnings, tables both small and large, sixty chairs, eight carpenters with their assorted tools, a large fine-mesh net, a barrel of rose petals, rolls of waterproofed canvas, buckets of nails and screws, the spit roast and all its turning mechanisms, braziers, bags of coal, ladders, four flags emblazoned with the duke's emblem, poles and base mountings, ninety coloured glass lamps and oil. Additionally, twelve soldiers from the royal guard in ceremonial dress and the twenty-four oarsmen who would row everything there and act as porters and labourers.

By early afternoon, everything had been transported from the waterside to the square. Then everyone stopped for a late lunch unpacked from two wooden trunks which they had brought with them, consisting of bread, cheeses, various cold meats, pears, and freshwater, which they ate and shared with the locals under the lime trees.

At three, Fra Paciolli started organising what should go where. The carpenters had already been given their plans and began by constructing the stage on the south-eastern side and the labourers laid out the long tables and assembled the spit roast with its racks, pulleys and turning wheels.

At six-thirty the plans for the square were taking shape and Fra Paciolli decided that was enough for the day so everyone returned to the barges, apart from the twelve soldiers. They would take it turns to keep an eye on what had been delivered, although no one expected any trouble except perhaps a little over inquisitiveness from the children which might lead to an accident.

The soldiers took it in three watches with those who were not on duty resting or sleeping on mattresses laid out on the church floor.

At seven-thirty the following day, only one barge was needed to carry Fra Paciolli, Luca, the carpenters, and its eight oarsmen, and when they had moored, only the commander stayed with the barge.

Soon the small stage was erected with a red canvas awning above it. After that, the long tables had poles fastened to each corner. On top of which, at either side were triangular frames and a bar connecting them covered in red canvas, the result looked like a market stall. The oil lamps were filled and placed in the six trees, the braziers filled with coal, the small tables and chairs arranged, the flags put atop of their poles one in each corner, and the fine mesh net was put up above the church door.

After a final inspection and when all was to his liking, Fra Paciolli left the square mid-afternoon and returned on the waiting barge to the palace.

On Friday, Christos who had worked quickly and almost constantly so as not dwell on the wedding and being apart from Angelica, had transferred his drawing to the panel and was satisfied with what he saw.

As he sat there looking at what he had done, a sinking feeling arose in the pit of his stomach, he had no best man to be by his side and pass him the rings. He stood, paced the room, sat down again, looked at the floor, stood again and left the house.

In the palace, Master Carlucci had been organising the entertainment and there was a lot to consider. The boar for the spit roast had been killed and was hanging in the cold rooms of the kitchens, the chickens were crated up and the orders for the other foods had been given to the head chef and sent out. The performers had already been informed and they were to assemble by ten on the Saturday of the wedding at the palace.

Christos had bolted out the door and headed for the palace, after a moment a voice said to him, "Slow down, what is the rush? Everything is going to be alright, you have trusted in me for a while now so do not fret or panic, solutions are always found to problems and remember what you have no control over is not a problem."

Arriving at the palace, he was shown into the library where he found the duke writing.

Looking up, the duke said, "I keep a diary and have done since a young boy and so did my father. I have read some of his and you are mentioned on many occasions with great affection."

Then as he blotted the ink, he asked the page, who was still in the doorway, to bring a bottle of sweet wine, two glasses and a plate of almond biscuits.

"Now please, Christos, sit and tell me why you are here."

"I not sure how to start but I have never made many friends, it is not something that I find easy. Painting can be a solitary life where one can be quite isolated," Christos hesitated, "But I wonder, would you be my best man?"

"Of course I would be delighted, it did cross my mind as to who you would ask but I assumed you had it arranged. I will tell you something, being in my position, it is also very difficult to make friends, people see my power and influence and wish to become close to me for no other reason, so in some ways, you and I are well matched."

The page knocked and put the tray down and the duke and Christos whiled away the afternoon.

The morning of the wedding was warm with a gentle breeze coming up from the south. The late summer was still with them but once the wind changed direction, it rarely went back again, then winter wouldn't be far away.

Christos had been invited to stay at the palace overnight so he could leave for the church with the duke. From his room, he watched as Master Carlucci conducted affairs at the waterfront, vessels large and small were loaded with all the people and things necessary for the celebration and then they slowly set sail for the square where he would marry Angelica.

An hour later Christos went downstairs and was met by the duke.

"It is time for us to go," the duke said.

Their barge contained the more important guests from the court and the duke's wife and moored at the nearest point to the church. The other vessels were already there and were still laden with their goods and people, all except for the musicians who had made their way through the alleys, taken up their positions on the stage and were already playing.

Everyone disembarked from the duke's barge and started walking, almost in procession, to the church. Christos was doing likewise when the duke took him by the arm and said, "No, we are going to take the longer route and enter the church from the rear, if we go with my wife and the others, those in the square will wave and welcome me and that would not be right because it is yours and Angelica's day."

So the two of them set off alone, following the path along the waterway to the next main mooring point. They then turned north-east and after a short while, came to a small courtyard and entered the church through the back door and went into the vestry.

No one seemed to notice them for a few moments, until they were almost in their seats at the front of the church when the duke turned and smiled at his wife.

Behind them, the church was filling up and Christos glanced around, looking down the aisle past those seated in the pews and through the open doors. He could see the crowd filling the square beyond and hoped Angelica was alright.

Mondino had been with Angelica all morning, he wanted to make sure she was relaxed and reassured from any anxieties, though actually she had none, but strangely, he had.

She had two maids, both friends since childhood wearing similar dresses to herself in deep pink satin, although hers had pearls in clusters sown over it.

The one-eyed Maria fussed over the three of them making final adjustments with pins and stitches of white thread, while Mondino, dressed in purple breeches, white ruffled shirt and a deep blue jacket, sat in a chair sipping a lemon liqueur he had come across in the kitchen. Removing his nerves, he said to himself.

There was a knock at her door and the little face of a chorister looked around it. "It is time," he said to the first person he saw, which was Mondino and off he scuttled.

The physician stirred himself and went into the room where the women were. "Are you ready?" he said, smiling at Angelica.

"Yes," she said.

Taking her arm, he led her out into the square where clapping immediately started from the assembled crowd. In the few steps it took from her house to the church, he said quietly, "I am very proud to be giving you away today, you look absolutely beautiful. I will tell you this, I never had children but, sweet Angelica, as I have told you before, I think of you as my daughter."

As they walked up the aisle, everyone turned around to look but she kept her poise and there ahead, Father Roberto with his huge rock-like frame was waiting, smiling.

The service seemed to go quickly, the duke passed the rings, Father Roberto gave them their vows, Christos and Angelica accepted them and then they kissed.

Of course, everyone smiled and gave their best wishes as they walked back down the aisle as husband and wife. Then at the door, they paused and kissed again at which the throng in the square once more broke into applause. As the musicians to their left started playing, a thin cord was tugged by someone out of sight and the fine net that had been put above the door opened and thousands of rose petals cascaded down on their heads and on the slight breeze, fluttered like butterflies all over the square.

While the wedding had been taking place, the tables in the square had been stocked out with all the various foods and drinks that Master Carlucci had arranged.

Now he ordered the spit roast to be lit for he had not wanted the aroma of it wafting into the church while the service was on.

Within a very short time the tables serving beer from wooden barrels, wine, either red or white, or cordial either orange, lime or lemon were busy with people ferrying back and forth eager for a drink.

There were also tables stacked high with small pies, some meat and some cheese, another table was equally full of small almond cakes coated in sugar. There was a pot of boiling oil that long strips of twisted dough were dipped into and then laid out and cut into suitable lengths then sprinkled with sugar, these and the almond cakes were particularly popular with the children, and all these foods kept everyone happy till the time when the hog and chickens were cooked and the main meal could be served but that would not be for a while.

The food on the other tables were being kept warm in large dishes that rested on platters with hot coals in them. They were full of such food as the vegetable or fish soups which were gently simmering away, or the desserts, from which you could choose either quinces in pastry served in wedges, baked apples stuffed with raisins and spices or pears and plums cooked in red wine.

Although it was not yet dark, two men with wooden spills attached to long thin poles started lighting the coloured glass lanterns hanging in the trees. When that had been done, they went around the square lighting the braziers while the musicians on the stage played and were joined by a singer who sang local songs.

With the happy feeling of the wedding, combined with the wine and beer and lovely food, couples started to dance along with Christos and Angelica. The duke and his wife, with no one paying them much heed, were bumped into several times by other dancers.

As night fell, the coloured-glass lamps swayed gently in the trees, the brazier's glowed sending little golden sparks into the air and the spit roast was ready, so the dancing stopped, the band took a rest and everyone found somewhere to sit and enjoy the wedding meal.

When the food was all gone and everyone felt satisfied, the music started up again, and now that it was dark the other entertainers joined in. A fire swallower stood on the church steps and amazed everybody, jugglers walked amongst the tables picking up plates, knives and forks, and kept them spinning in the air as if by magic.

It was a night like no other for the square and those that lived in it and Christos and Angelica couldn't have felt happier.

Chapter Twenty

Two months later winter had arrived, the wind from the mountains in the north cut its icy chill through whatever one wore.

"The snow will be here soon," Christos said as he heard Angelica enter from the kitchen behind him. "Then maybe it will be a little warmer."

She placed a log on the fire and stood by his side looking at the picture for Father Roberto's church. "It is almost finished," she said.

Turning to her, Christos said, "I love you more with every day that passes. You are woven into me, you are part of me." Gently squeezing her hand, he returned his attention to the painting.

Early the following morning, before it was light and with Angelica nestled by his side sleeping soundly, Christos heard a familiar voice within him.

"You have changed everything, have you not? Four seasons have barely passed and the black monster is but a distant memory and you did it by opening the windows of yourself and letting in some light. You changed your negative thoughts and actions and put right the wrongs you had done. You got rid of anger, bitterness, jealousy and all those other bad feelings you thought were you, and so stopped hating yourself.

"It took courage, remember how afraid at first you were but nothing terrible happened to you, did it? Then you started to take care of yourself, and after that, you started to care for others and see their needs instead of only yours. You swapped arrogance for humility and applied integrity to what you undertook and it did not make you weaker only stronger.

"Then you started to see what you had been blind too, namely the woman lying by your side who cared and loved you, and then the children who had so little, and this you did shortly after you thought there was no future for you. Now you have changed the future of more than just yourself by giving, and in so doing have brought happiness to many, which by your actions will ripple forever outwards like a pebble thrown in a pond.

"These things, this course of action you have taken, was why I became yours, I helped you realise your dreams but you lost your way. I was always here, even though you forgot me, and when everything seemed to go wrong and you lost your faith, we together put it right.

"While I have your attention, let me tell you something about myself. I, as I'm sure you realised, am very old. I remember countries and places that have long since gone. I remember when vast teeming rivers were tiny streams, and when desserts were green and fertile valleys, and forests were hard and rocky soil. I can recall mountains that are no more, and islands that are now at the bottom of the sea; and I have seen virgin land formed. In fact, I have seen all the change there has been, and I will see as much again and more.

"The span of your life, whatever it turns out to be, will last no more than the flash of sunlight on a wave as it breaks upon the shore. That does not mean it is not important judged against the endlessness of time, but the exact opposite. You have a responsibility to use the energy within your body of skin and bone to improve not only yourself but, if you can, everyone else. Some people achieve this and they become beacons of what we can be, a testament to the human spirit.

"It is also my belief that the energy you now have will travel with you through your death and into your next life, and the better energy you carry with you the more complete your next life will be, but here at this time, there is no need to talk of such things.

"As you know, on my front are shapes and patterns in different colours, they are symbols. Over time they have been attached to me by different peoples, with different tongues and customs, but they are ultimately all the same. They express balance and harmony within yourself and with the world around you, and if you have those qualities you will care and love both yourself and everything else. Now rest and dream for soon another seed of your life will ripen which in a sense will bring it full circle."

There was a silence as Christos woke and wrapped a gown around himself, walking to the window. The scene outside was white, it had snowed, thick deep snow that the wind had here and there pushed and moulded into rounded drifts against walls and doorways and any other obstacle it had come across during the dark hours.

He reflected on the words that had come to his mind during the night and wondered for a moment what awaited him as he watched the final few snowflakes fall out of the pale grey sky.

Turning away from the window, he went down to the kitchen and put the kettle on to boil for a warming tea. He put fresh logs on the fires and with the tea made, returned upstairs to wake Angelica.

There was no new snowfall over the next two days, it melted a little during the day and froze again at night. Late on the second afternoon, Christos needed some air. Angelica was reading and content near the fire but he wanted a short walk and so went out alone.

Underfoot was slippery so he walked with care and kept away from the water's edge. There was a moon, a luminous waxing crescent whose light gave clues as to where it might be icy. No one was out as the daylight was about to go, whatever people needed to do, they had done; even the little eating place he saw as he passed its windows had no more than three people inside.

He began to feel the cold on his hands and fingers which he buried deep in his pockets and on his face, the skin tightened from the chill; but he felt good for being out.

After ten minutes or so, he thought he heard an odd sound and stopped so that the crunching of ice and snow did not interfere with what it might be. At first, he thought it was the wind playing in the rigging of one of the boats moored alongside the quay but this he soon dismissed as the sound seemed musical.

He walked on a little way as a hunter might do, with a degree of stealth, trying to pinpoint the sounds which were undoubtedly music. Still not discerning where the sounds were coming from, Christos rounded a grain warehouse located in a part of the city which even in summer seemed bleak and unadorned.

There at the side of a wooden footbridge where a small waterway joined the main one, stood a figure playing a pipe. Christos was some forty paces away from the piper in the shadows and what he heard standing there, were sounds that seemed as natural and more in tune with the moon and stars above than the wind itself.

He stood and listened while time stood still until the playing stopped. Then in a sudden violent movement accompanied by a primaeval scream, the figure threw the pipe as far away from himself as he could into the iced water.

Christos drew in his breath at what he saw and was brought back to the chill evening around him. Watching what was happening in front of him, he saw the figure drop to its knees and where there was a moment ago a figure playing the most exquisite sounds, there now appeared what seemed no more than a pile of crumpled rags.

Squinting his eyes against the chill wind and to focus on what he was seeing, Christos walked towards the shape upon the ground.

When he was ten or so paces away, he heard it crying, "My friend, what is wrong?" Christos asked.

The crying stopped and a voice said, "Go away, just leave, I do not want your attention, just go."

Christos, ignoring the request, sat down on the cold ground and placed an arm on the shoulder of the figure. He shrugged with no real intent but almost symbolically and said, "I am not leaving. I listened to you playing, it was beautiful. Why did you throw the pipe away?"

"I cannot tell you," the figure replied. "And you would not understand if I did."

"I think you may not be right about that, my friend," Christos replied. Looking up, he saw that the pipe had not, as he had thought, sunk to the bottom of the waterway but was lying on top of a slab of ice that was ever so slowly moving under the bridge.

Quick as a flash, he ran to the point where the bridge met the land, removed his coat and using it in a sweeping movement, flicked the pipe close to him and picked it up.

"I have saved your pipe."

"I do not care, I have vowed never to play it again," said the figure, shaking with both inner pain and cold.

"Fine, do not play it again that is your choice, but I am not going to allow you to freeze to death."

Putting his arm around the shivering figure, he lifted him off the ground. Christos had expected a heavier weight, a body with more substance, but this person seemed to weigh nothing, just skin and bone, and he could feel the weakness of the body next to him that needed supporting.

"What may I call you? My name is Christos."

"Gulli, you can call me Gulli."

When they reached Moon Street, Christos took the large key from his pocket, turned it in the lock and opened the door.

"Angelica, I am back," he called.

She appeared at the top of the stairs and seeing her surprise at the figure by his side, he said, "This is Gulli, I met him on my walk and he seemed to have got a little lost so I thought I would invite him around for dinner. I remembered you made some chicken, leek, and dumpling stew, is that alright?"

Angelica was no fool and could see that this man Gulli was a waif, and his clothes with the torn arm on his coat confirmed it to her eyes. Smiling she said, "Of course, there is plenty. Gulli, you are more than welcome."

"Thank you," he said. "You are very kind."

Angelica took his coat from him and placed it in the kitchen to dry and with only a look she said to Christos, *what is going on? Where did you find him*? For the coat was virtually sodden.

Then knowing that he too must be soaked and cold, she said, "The stew needs another thirty to forty minutes to be at its best, and as it is such a bitter night to have been out, I will draw you a bath, Gulli, before we eat."

Giving Gulli no opportunity to object or protest, she went about the task.

"Come sit near the fire while she makes your bath," Christos said.

"She is a lovely woman and you are both very kind."

"It is nothing my friend," Christos said. And as the hard lines of the cold in the man's face started to soften, he saw how very young this man was, almost a boy.

"This is a beautiful house and I see that you are an artist."

"Yes, it is, and I am very fortunate to live here. I am indeed an artist. It is what I have always wanted to do and the fates have been very good to me."

At that, Gulli looked down as if the weight of his thoughts left him nowhere else to look. Christos stood and leaving for a moment, went to the kitchen. Returning, he said, "Here drink this, it is made by the monks at a monastery. It is distilled wine and will take the chill from your insides."

Sipping the drink and with the proximity of the fire, the young man's colour started to return to his face.

"The bath is ready," Angelica said with a kind authority Christos had never heard before. "I have put out dry clean clothes for you to wear, and I want you to put your damp clothes outside the bathroom door as quickly as you can so I can start drying them."

Gulli was in no condition to argue as Angelica showed him the way and outside the door, she said, "I'll wait here for your clothes."

"Where did you find him?" she asked. Christos retold the events of his walk while Angelica listened and looked thoughtful but said only, "We will have supper and then I will make up a bed for him."

A short time later, Gulli returned, dressed in fresh, clean clothes.

"You look better," Christos said. "Come and sit, you must be hungry. My wife's stews are excellent."

Conversation was minimal but that was alright, Gulli's hunger was plain to see and when Angelica offered more stew there was no objection, but before the second bowl was finished, Gulli was asleep, his head on his arm across the table.

When Angelica had made up the bed that had once been Jacamo's at the front of the house, Christos carefully lifted Gulli's skinny body away from the table and half carried, half dragged him onto the bed.

He removed the one slipper that had remained on, placed the covers over him, drew the curtains and then giving him a final look, closed the door, leaving him to sleep.

"He plays the flute wonderfully," he said, taking the pipe he had retrieved off the ice from his coat. "I tell you, I have never heard such exquisite sounds played on this instrument in my life."

"But why did he throw his pipe away and why was he crying?" Angelica asked.

"I do not know, perhaps he will tell us tomorrow."

Rain was falling when Christos looked out of the window the following morning, and he could tell it was very cold rain which gave him extra pleasure to be inside.

He made tea and took it back to bed, kissing Angelica on the arm who stirred from beneath the depths of the bedding.

"Is he awake yet?" she said after a few moments.

"I stopped outside his door but heard nothing."

The morning passed with Angelica going quickly to the market to get vegetables, cheese and some bread rolls while Christos worked on the altarpiece.

At midday, they sat down to eat with the logs crackling on the fire when Gulli appeared.

"You slept well I hope," said Christos. "Come and join us."

Angelica fetched another plate, glass and knife.

"Thank you, I slept very well but I must be moving on, I have things to attend to."

"Well your clothes are still damp," Angelica said when clearing the table. "So you will have to wait a while."

When Angelica had left them, Christos said, "You have nowhere to go, my friend, or anything to attend to. I do not know you but I know more about you than you may think. I saw the state you were in last night and I know that state myself. You threw away what was precious to you, could see no tomorrow and you were enveloped with despair and blackness."

Christos smiled and poured Gulli another glass of wine and said, "I know what that is like, I have lived in the place you feel you are in, so be brave, be courageous, and tell me something of how I came to find you half-frozen and desolate last night."

"I have, I feel, nothing to lose," Gulli said. "As I have nothing to lose and you and your wife have been so very good to me, I will tell you my story. I have practised and played the pipe since I was a small boy. My parents were not rich so we had very little and I do not come from this country. We arrived here when I was still young because in my land there was a war and we had no choice but to flee. My mother became a maid, my father found work but it was hard for him. They both died some time ago. I have no skills except the ability to play the flute and the pipe. I have done many menial jobs and tried with all the efforts I could summon to make a living from my music, but for whatever reason the stars above have not been kind to me. The only work I have found is playing in bars where no one really listens or standing on street corners, sometimes not making enough coins for that day.

"Last night, when you came upon me I felt without hope, and in some way tricked by this world into thinking I could have a future in doing what I love, so I decided I was not going to play a part in destiny's game with me anymore and threw my flute away.

"Had you not been there, I would probably have done the same with myself. Today my body feels rested and cared for but I will tell you, my heart feels no different to how it did, so when my clothes are dry, I must leave and see which way the winds take me."

Christos refilled both glasses without saying a word, and Gulli noticed a seriousness in his host he had not seen before.

"I said that I knew you better than you might think," said Christos. "I will tell you why. Your state yesterday was my state not so long ago. Our reasons for arriving there were different but we both ended in the same place, with the same despair, the same feeling of there being no point to the future, the same sense of utter dejection. You thought yesterday that only you in this whole wide world felt so badly but unfortunately, that was just not true. There are many many people from the north to the south and from the east to the west, who speak in every tongue, and are of every colour, that at this very moment, see no light to reach for, no point in breathing anymore, and a lot will not have the good fortune to pull back from the brink.

"They will kill themselves, they will snuff out the flame that was them, and the sun will never rise like a golden disc in the morning sky, nor the moon shine with its silvery light in their eyes again, but for you, for them, as there was for me, there is an answer, a way of turning your blackness into light."

Gulli sat listening. He was still exhausted but the fear and adrenalin that had kept him going for so long were gone and he was in a new place, a place where he was meant to hear these words.

"You feel," Christos said, "That life has dealt you bad cards, that whatever you do will make no difference but you are wrong.

Leave the past behind, stop bringing the misfortunes and mistakes that happened in your yesterdays into today, now, this moment, is all that matters."

Gulli listened quietly, sipping his wine.

"Stop carrying your past into the future, stop looking for what is wrong and finding fault and think of what is right, you know that everything will pass, even the tallest mountain will one day be a handful of dust. That is not a thought that should be negative but a thought to remind you to take nothing for granted because whatever you think will, like the mountain, one day be no more, it will have gone. So accept and enjoy what you have, do not reject good things or praise that comes your way because it is what you are meant to have, it is yours, and if you stop fighting your situation, everything will be alright. So open the windows of yourself and let what is around you enter and then almost as if by magic, energy will return to you in an ever-increasing way and the days of blackness will be gone, they will be your yesterdays and not your now.

"I know at this moment, sitting here at this table on a winter's afternoon, you are thinking nothing has changed and that tomorrow will be as hard as yesterday, but again you will see you are wrong. Today was almost as if it was day one, a new start. You will see."

Gulli said nothing and accepted the next glass of wine.

"I have something for you," Christos said, and going to his coat draped over a chair, pulled out the pipe. "Here, this is yours, I know you never wanted to see it again but it seems it was not meant to leave you."

Gulli took it with an ironic smile and laying it on the table in front of him, studied it almost as if he had no idea what it was or what it did.

Christos walked to the window. "If you are set on leaving, I suggest you wait till tomorrow as night has now arrived and the snow is again falling, but I am also going to ask you a favour before you leave, I would like you to play one of your tunes for my wife. Would that be asking too much?"

"Of course not," Gulli replied and for the first time since Christos had seen him, Gulli sounded positive.

Gulli continued, "You have both been kinder to me than I ever imagined people could be, and yes I would like to stay."

Neither man had said anything to Angelica about Christos' request while they ate dinner, which was chickpeas with fish and onions in a thick white wine stock.

"That meal was delicious, you are a wonderful cook and as a thank you and as a way of repaying you, I would like to play you some music."

"I can think of nothing better. I would be delighted to hear you play," Angelica replied.

Gulli started playing, at first some simple well-known melodies, then more complicated ones that seemed to push the pipe to its limits for such a simple instrument, but all were played with a beautifully sweet and full sound.

Angelica almost broke into laughter with the joy and excitement of what she heard and could not restrain herself from clapping when he had finished. "That was wonderful, just wonderful," she said.

Gulli did not leave but stayed on in the house, helping out with things. Christos provided fresh clothes and Angelica warm meals.

The weather was still cold but the driving rain had cleared the snow. Four days later a knock on the door revealed one of the duke's pages.

Gulli, who had answered, bought the sealed papers up to Christos who was still working on the altarpiece for Father Roberto.

Christos knew it was from the duke and breaking the seal, saw he and Angelica had been invited to the annual banquet on the evening of the solstice just a few days away. It had been two years since he had last attended and the event held a special place in his memories.

"Gulli we have been invited to the palace for a celebration and I would like you to come with us, how do you feel about that?"

"Thank you, it would be an honour," Gulli replied.

On the afternoon of the banquet at the time arranged, a barge collected the three of them from the waterfront door of Moon Street.

Christos could see Gulli's apprehension as the barge made its slow way across the city, stopping and picking up other guests. To reassure him and quell his nervousness, Christos told of his past times at this event, how on one evening it had elevated him from being a humble apprentice, and on another, his good self had left him and he had behaved appallingly.

When they arrived, the usual flares and braziers lit the entrance to the palace and Christos held Angelica's hand as for her, this was also something new and slightly daunting.

They were shown through to the great hall, which was beginning to fill. As they looked around for those they knew, the duke appeared.

"Good evening, I am so pleased to see you both, my wife and I would like you both to join us and sit with us through the evening as our special guests."

"That would be an honour and a pleasure but I have taken the liberty of bringing with us a new acquaintance, let me introduce Gulli who is a truly wonderful musician we have had the fortune to meet."

"Fortune indeed," the duke replied. "Antonio, the composer of all the music in the palace and of our music here tonight, is in a bit of a state. His flute player has come down with a sudden illness, not serious but our highly-strung Antonio is worried. You, Gulli," taking him by the arm and leading him away, "will quiet our music master's nerves."

Christos and Angelica watched from across the room as Gulli was introduced to Antonio and the others in the ensemble and soon they were going through rehearsals of the night's music and the young man who so recently had almost frozen to death, seemed totally at home and had a smile on his face.

Christos and Angelica did not stay late and before they left, they went over to Gulli during an interval and asked if he was alright and told him they were going home.

"I have not been this happy since I do not know when," Gulli replied. "Master Antonio has asked me to stay on after the banquet is finished so we in the ensemble can have our own celebration."

"Well enjoy the rest of the evening and we'll see you back at Moon Street whenever you are finished here."

Two days later Gulli returned and on entering the studio he looked as pleased as could be.

"Welcome back," Christos said. "It looks as if you had a good time."

"It could not have gone better. Master Antonio has asked me to stay on and become part of his musicians and I have been given a room at the palace, so yes all is very good and it is thanks to you, Christos," and he gave him a hug.

At that moment, Angelica came in from the kitchen, "I could not help overhearing what you said." She gave him a squeeze and a kiss on the cheek that embarrassed him, but in a good way.

Gulli stayed for lunch, a simple meal of vegetable soup and bread. When it was over, he started expressing his gratitude for all they had both done for him, when Christos said, "Wait a moment," and left the room.

On returning, he said, "Here, this is for you," and gave Gulli a package wrapped in yellowing canvas.

A little surprised, Gulli unwrapped the package and in it was the cloak. "I don't know what to say."

"There is no need to say anything," Christos said.

"It was mine for a while and before that someone else's, and down through the years, it has passed from person to person. It came to me because I needed it, although there were times I did not deserve it, and now it is in your keeping. When life gets difficult it will help you. I know you do not fully understand what I am telling you but you will, now go my friend and have a good life."

Ex tenebris venit lux

Out of darkness cometh light.

A Message from the Author

Thank you for reading *The Cloak,* I hope you enjoyed it. This is my debut novel but you can keep an eye out for my second book, an anthology of poems, short stories and novellas.

If you feel so inclined, I would greatly appreciate it if you could write a review on Amazon. It only takes a minute and gives other potential readers a better idea of what the book is like.

You can follow me on Instagram @jamesghussey where I post my art and if you would like to get in touch or give me any feedback, you can email me on jamesghussey@gmail.com.

Printed in Great Britain
by Amazon

62060169R00132